Before
the
Story

3 BOOKS IN 1

Disney
Before the Story

3 BOOKS IN 1

Elsa's Icy Rescue

By **KATE EGAN**

ILLUSTRATED BY **MARIO CORTES**

Tiana's Best Surprise

By **TESSA ROEHL**

ILLUSTRATED BY **ARIANNA REA**

Cinderella Takes the Stage

By **TESSA ROEHL**

ILLUSTRATED BY **ADRIENNE BROWN**

Disney PRESS

Los Angeles • New York

Published by Disney Press, an imprint of Buena Vista Books, Inc.
No part of this book may be reproduced or transmitted in any form or by any means, electronic or mechanical, including photocopying, recording, or by any information storage and retrieval system, without written permission from the publisher. For information address Disney Press, 1200 Grand Central Avenue, Glendale, California 91201.

Printed in the United States of America

Elsa's Icy Rescue, First Paperback Edition, March 2020

Tiana's Best Surprise originally published by Random House Children's Books, First Paperback Edition, January 2018

Cinderella Takes the Stage originally published by Random House Children's Books, First Paperback Edition, January 2017

First Bind-Up Edition, September 2021

10 9 8 7 6 5 4 3 2 1

FAC-029261-21204

Library of Congress Control Number: 2021930897

ISBN 978-1-368-07332-5

For more Disney Press fun, visit www.disneybooks.com

DISNEY

Before the Story

Elsa's ICY RESCUE

BY
KATE EGAN

ILLUSTRATED BY
MARIO CORTES

Chapter 1
The Sommerhus

As the royal carriage made its way past rows of tall pines, Elsa felt far from home. All she could hear was the steady *clomp, clomp* of the white horses' hooves and the call of distant birds. Oh, yes, and the voice of her little sister, Anna. "Are we there yet?" Anna said every few minutes. "Are we almost there?"

It was summertime, and Elsa's family were making their annual trip to the Sommerhus, a quaint cottage in a small village just outside the Arendelle forest. Every summer, they left the castle behind and stayed a few weeks alone at the cottage, without castle staff or royal responsibilities.

Back home in Arendelle, Elsa spent every day preparing for the distant future when she would become queen. She spent hours with the castle governess in the schoolroom, reviewing the names of past rulers and going over royal etiquette. At the Sommerhus, though, she did not have to think about her future at all. While they were away, they could be just a normal family and Elsa could be just a normal girl.

Elsa's mother, Queen Iduna, looked out the window as the carriage passed another row of trees outside. She breathed in deeply and said, "Don't you love the smell of cedar?"

"I think we're almost there!" Anna cried. She twisted toward the carriage window and pointed at a path paved with pebbles. "Yes, this is where we turn!"

Elsa's father, King Agnarr, extended his arm to make sure Anna didn't tumble out the window. "It's still a little farther," he said. "Just be patient—we'll be there in no time."

Catching her sister's eye, Elsa smiled.

Who could be patient when they were getting so close?

Her mind raced, thinking about everything their trip would hold. Elsa loved the feeling of being alone with her family at the edge of the forest. She looked forward to all their summer traditions—playing games and making music and hiking through the hills. There would be new adventures, too, of course, and Elsa could only wonder what they would be.

The carriage pitched forward as it went over a bump in the road. Suddenly, Elsa knew just where they were. "This is it!" she said, leaning across the carriage to hug her sister as the road wound past a wooden stave church in a tiny village. She knew every inch of the rest of the way.

They went around another bend, moving through the town square and approaching a cobblestone path. At the end of the road, Elsa could see their cheerful cottage, with its sturdy log walls and bright red trim. The window boxes were planted with pink and white flowers, and the grass was freshly cut. The Sommerhus was just as friendly and welcoming as Elsa remembered it.

As soon as the carriage stopped, the girls leaped out and ran to the heavy front door. Anna pushed and pushed, but she couldn't get it open until Elsa stepped up beside her to lend an extra hand. "One, two, three!" the sisters counted. And the door to their summer adventures swung wide open.

Elsa stepped into the cottage and circled around, taking it all in.

First she saw the long wooden table where her family would gather for their meals. Behind it was a grandfather clock that had belonged to Elsa's own grandfather and the large fireplace that warmed the cottage when the nights grew cool. In every corner, there were stacks of favorite books and games. On a narrow shelf near the ceiling were the beautiful plates Elsa's mother had collected on her travels as queen. And hanging on the wall were the fiddles her father played in the evening. Everything was just as she remembered.

Elsa grabbed Anna by the hand and pulled her up the stairs, taking them two at a time. "Let's go see our room!" she said.

At the cottage, Anna and Elsa shared a room under the eaves. It was small and dark, and some nights they could hear the sound of raindrops pounding against the roof. This was where Elsa had her happiest dreams.

Elsa walked into the room and stretched out on her bed. On the other side of the room, Anna bounced on her mattress. "Let's go exploring!" she said.

But Elsa was not ready to explore. She wanted to soak in the feeling of being inside the Sommerhus at last. Fortunately, she knew something that would keep Anna occupied for a little while. "Not yet," she said. "But look at this."

On Elsa's side of the room was a small wooden trunk with pink trim. She hopped off her bed, crouched, and lifted the lid, its hinges squeaking.

Inside the trunk were the toys the girls

played with only at the Sommerhus. Eight-year-old Elsa had nearly outgrown the building blocks and spinning tops, but there were some toys she would never get too old for. Tucked carefully at the bottom of the trunk, covered with soft blankets, was a pair of well-loved dolls. Elsa lifted one out as if it was an old friend. The doll had blond braids and bright blue eyes. Elsa hugged it and said, "Good to see you, Hildy!"

"Hanna! Hanna!" Anna cried, edging her sister out of the way. She pulled the other doll from the trunk and lifted it into the air. "We're back!" This doll had red hair the same shade as Anna's. Anna lifted Hildy from Elsa's arms. In no time, she was changing both dolls into their summer dresses.

Returning to her bed and lying back on her pillow, Elsa sighed and smiled.

Elsa would miss some things about the castle while they were gone, of course, but the Sommerhus felt like home to her. Not only was it the place she got to spend time with her family and take a break from her lessons, but it was where she could be herself—her *whole* self. At the Sommerhus, she didn't have to hide her magic.

Since she'd been there last, Elsa had learned more about her astonishing power. Whenever she wanted, she could create ice and snow. Well . . . sort of. Until she knew how to use her power properly, she had to keep it out of sight. At the Sommerhus, no one outside the family would see her—and no one would stop her—so she could test the limits of her magic.

Chapter 2
A Walk in the Woods

"**A**fter you finish unpacking, who's ready for a walk to the fjord?" Queen Iduna called from downstairs. The sisters were putting their clothes and bags away. The dolls, Hildy and Hanna, waited patiently on the windowsill.

"We're ready right now!" Elsa called back. The sisters hurried down the steps to join their mother.

The sky was blue and the sun bright as Anna and Elsa followed their parents into the afternoon. A trip to the sparkling fjord was always a highlight of the family's first day away from home.

Queen Iduna led the way behind the cottage and to a hidden path near the edge of the forest. The path wove around some tall trees, and soon the cottage was out of sight. The family was alone with the wonders of nature.

Elsa wondered what people in Arendelle would say if they could see their queen right then. Her mother was practically skipping along the path. "I can't wait to put my toes in the water," she said. Elsa giggled. Her mother sounded like Anna.

Her father was watching the sky intently. "Could that be a hawk?" he wondered aloud, pointing at something as it swooped over-head. Not many people knew that the king had a special interest in birds.

The grassy path gave way to a rougher trail studded with stones, leading up a gentle incline. As the family climbed higher, there were some larger rocks in their way. Anna and Elsa raced around them, and soon the girls were ahead of their parents.

"Don't touch the ground!" Anna dared Elsa. This was one of their favorite games.

Instead of stepping directly on the trail, the girls hopped from stone to stone. If there were no stones, they walked on roots or tree stumps or clumps of leaves—anything to avoid the ground.

Anna reached a stretch of trail with nothing else to step on. The only way to avoid the ground was to swing from a tree branch like a monkey.

When Elsa got to that same part of the trail, she decided to do something else. Sure, she could swing like a monkey . . . or she could avoid the ground in her *own* way.

Elsa looked around to make sure no one outside her family was around. Then she stretched out her hands and waved them over the path. She could feel her magic building, but she never quite knew what was about to happen. Would it work? Elsa held her breath. But in no time, the ground was covered by a thin sheet of ice about as long as she was tall,

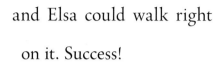

and Elsa could walk right on it. Success!

Anna looked back and saw the ice glinting in a patch of sunlight. "No fair!" she said. "That's against the rules!" But Anna also saw the possibility for fun. She raced toward Elsa and took a flying leap onto the ice, gliding from one end to the other.

"Too bad I don't have my ice skates," Anna said. There wasn't enough ice for skating, but as Elsa slid to the edge of the ice and continued on, she wondered if she could make more next time.

By the time their parents came up the trail, the thin layer of ice had melted to a trickle in the heat and the girls had scrambled even farther ahead. Elsa was near the top of the hill when she heard her mother's voice through the trees.

"Anna! Elsa!" she called.

Soon her father chimed in. "Wherever you are, stop and wait for us!"

It was only a few minutes before King Agnarr and Queen Iduna reached their daughters, but the king seemed worried. "Please don't get too far ahead," he said. "It's important that we all stay together for safety's sake."

Just ahead, the trail ended at a bluff. The whole family walked together until they reached the very best view in the kingdom. From the top of the bluff, they could see a wide vista of shining blue water, with snow-covered mountains in the distance. The fjord was dotted with colorful boats and a few rocky islands covered in pine. Elsa took a deep breath. There was no place she would rather be.

The queen scrambled down the bluff toward the water and the sandy shore, calling "Follow me!" It was tradition for the girls and their mother to wade in the water before the end of their first day at the Sommerhus.

Quickly, the three of them took off their shoes and dipped in their feet. "Too cold!" said Anna, running away from the water as soon as she felt its bite. Elsa waded in up to her ankles. She didn't mind the chill one bit.

After the dip in the water, Elsa and Anna made sand angels near the shore until it was time to go back to the cottage. Their mother led the way down the trail but stopped short. "Oh, how wonderful!" she cried, crouching in front of a bush. "Girls, come and see!" She plucked fresh strawberries off the bush and dropped them into her daughters' out-stretched hands. "Nature feeds our spirits *and* our bodies," she told Elsa and Anna.

"Look, there are more!" Elsa said, venturing away from the trail and into the forest. She could see many more strawberry bushes growing in the shadows.

But her father put a hand on her elbow. "Remember, Elsa. We need to stay together. There could be dangers hidden in the forest."

Elsa stepped back so as not to worry her father. With her power, though, came a growing confidence. Whatever dangers came her way, she would always have a means to face them.

Chapter 3
Building the Fort

That night, Elsa and Anna pushed their beds next to each other and curled up together under one big blanket. Elsa loved the cozy feeling of sleeping next to her sister. The only tricky part was the morning. At the castle, Anna could sleep all day if their parents let her. But at the Sommerhus, no matter how late she went to bed, Anna always woke up early. She was too excited to stay asleep!

So it was no surprise when Anna started tugging Elsa's arm at the faintest sign of dawn the next day. "Elsa!" she whispered. "Time to get up!"

Elsa pulled a pillow over her eyes and shrank beneath the blanket. Then she felt a gust of cold air as Anna peeled the blanket off her legs.

"Want to play?" Anna asked. "I have a great idea!"

Elsa sat up and hit her head on the low ceiling. "It's too early!" she said, rubbing her head.

"But we have to make a fort!" Anna explained. "I have it all figured out. I just need you to help me set it up."

"What do we need a fort for?" Elsa asked, yawning.

"It's for Hildy and Hanna!" Anna said. "They need a Sommerhus of their own."

Elsa fell back on the bed. It was impossible to say no to Anna, because she would continue to ask and ask until she got what she wanted. The first ray of sunshine pierced the room as Elsa sat up again, blinking. "Where do you think we should put it?"

Anna grinned and replied, "Right here." She patted the bed and gestured to a large blanket she had found that they could use for the fort's roof.

Elsa dragged some chairs over and placed them on either side of the two twin beds. Anna draped the blanket on top of them, and for a minute it was perfect—until the blanket began to sag. "I think we need to tie the blanket to the chairs," Elsa said. "That way it will stay put."

The girls knotted the blanket to the chairs with hair ribbons and pulled it tight, but the knots had a way of loosening after a few minutes. Could Elsa use her magic to fix this problem? After a few moments of intense concentration, she conjured up some bits of ice and froze the blanket to the chairs. Problem solved—at least until the ice melted.

"Watch out," Anna cautioned as she carried a pile of pillows across the room. From inside the fort, Elsa watched Anna stagger toward her, pillows teetering in her arms. They fell just as she reached the fort. Elsa crawled out, giggling, and took the pillows into the fort one by one.

"Hanna and Hildy are going to love it in here!" Elsa told her sister. But the fort wasn't only for the dolls, Elsa knew. She and Anna were going to love it in there, too. And the best part was that they had all day to play.

The only thing that could drag them out of the fort was the sound of their father's voice downstairs. "Time for breakfast!" he called.

By the time Elsa had gotten to her feet, Anna was already halfway down the stairs. Back home in Arendelle, King Agnarr never made breakfast. On their summer trip, though, he made pancakes every morning, and he had promised their favorite: pancakes with chocolate.

The long table was set with a purple tablecloth and a vase of wildflowers from their walk the day before. There was a pitcher of cold milk and a bottle of syrup that glowed like gold. Best of all, Elsa thought, one of her mother's special plates sat at each place.

Usually the plates were kept on a shelf, but they came out for important occasions, like their first breakfast together at the Sommerhus. Each plate was a memento from their parents' travels around the kingdom.

Elsa sat at the table. She picked up one of

her favorite plates—painted with a crocus—and flopped a pancake on top.

No one could see the design on Anna's plate because pancakes covered every inch. They were piled high and overflowing off the edge, and Anna splashed syrup over them with such force that drops flew across the table. When she poured her milk, some of it missed the glass and ended up on the floor.

"Elsa," her mother cautioned. Startled, Elsa looked up. Had her mother mixed up the sisters? Sometimes she did that, calling one by the other's name. In spite of Anna's mess, though, the queen was looking at *her*.

"Remember where to leave your knife after you cut your pan-cakes," her mother said. "It should rest on the side of your plate, not on the table."

Elsa looked at Anna, who was picking up a pancake with her fingers. Did her mother even notice?

"A future queen must watch her manners," Queen Iduna said. "That will be our project for today."

"We already have a project for today,"

Anna announced. "Wait until you see our fort."

Queen Iduna shook her head. "I'm afraid things will be a little different this year," she said. "Now that Elsa is getting older, we are going to keep up her lessons while we're here."

Elsa swallowed her last bite, though the pancake didn't taste quite as sweet anymore. *This isn't fair!* she thought. Their summer trip was the only time she didn't have to think about becoming queen.

What was the point of a trip with her family, Elsa wondered, if she would have to sit through all the same lessons she had at home? She wouldn't get to spend the morning playing with Anna after all. And not even her magic could change that.

Chapter 4
Lessons for Elsa

Anna gave Elsa a hug when she finished breakfast. "I won't play in the fort until you can come, too," she promised. Her syrupy hands stuck to Elsa's hair when she pulled away.

Elsa managed a small smile. "It's okay," she told her sister. "The lessons will fly by."

One of the first rules of being a ruler

was never to complain about ruling. But Elsa was disappointed.

While her father and Anna walked to the village, Elsa and her mother settled down in two big chairs in front of the fireplace. It was sunny outside, but a chill hung over the room.

Queen Iduna cleared her throat. "Let's get started by reviewing some of the material your teacher gave me to go over with you," she said, consulting the large book in her lap. "Do you remember the first ten rulers of Arendelle?"

Just like her routine back home, the day's

lessons started with a little history. Usually Elsa did her lessons with her governess, Miss Larson, but her mom had explained that she would be taking over Elsa's teaching while they were away. After all, her mom had taken the same lessons before she had become queen many years before, and who

better to teach Elsa how to be a proper ruler than the current queen of Arendelle?

Elsa kept her voice steady as she recited the past kings and queens. It was a long list of names, but Elsa remembered every single one.

"Very good!" Queen Iduna said when she was finished. "Shall we move on to the national treasures?"

Dutifully, Elsa described the national treasures of the kingdom. They were crowns and jeweled scepters, ceremonial robes, and special books that had been important to the family for centuries.

"Well done!" her mother said. "Soon you

will be ready to visit the vault where they are kept."

Elsa did not want to visit the vault. She did not want to do anything except finish the lesson. None of this was how she had imagined her time at the Sommerhus. But she knew that complaining would only make the lessons longer.

Queen Iduna seemed to sense Elsa's disinterest. After reviewing a few more national treasures, she said, "Let's finish today's lessons with something new and review proper place settings and table manners."

Her mother stood up and led the way back to the table where they had eaten breakfast. Thanks to King Agnarr, the mess had disappeared and the plates were neatly stacked after washing.

Queen Iduna took a clean plate off the top of the stack and laid it on the table in front of Elsa. "A formal meal is different from a family meal," she began. "First, let me show you how a place setting should look."

Elsa nodded.

"The plate is at the center," the queen said. Then she showed Elsa the proper place for everything else that would surround it on a table, from the napkin to the dessert plate. Elsa did not know there was supposed to be a special plate for dessert!

Forks, knives, spoons, glasses—Elsa knew what all those were used for. For a formal occasion, though, it turned out each place setting needed three forks, three spoons, and something called a finger bowl. "It will be filled with water," her mother explained. "And before dessert, your guests will dip their fingertips in to clean them."

"Like a bath?" Elsa asked. "Just for your fingers?"

Her mother smiled. "Exactly like a bath. But only for fingertips. First one hand, and then the other, but never the whole hand." Elsa bit her lip to keep from laughing. It all sounded so silly.

"And of course," Queen Iduna added, winking, "one must never drink the water. That is considered terribly rude."

The idea of someone drinking the finger-bowl water made Elsa crack up. "Like drinking from the bathtub?" she said, giggling.

Her mother ruffled her hair a little. "Just like that," she said. "See how much you have already learned today?"

Elsa frowned. She knew her mother was right, but there was so much more that Elsa needed to know.

Finally, she asked, "But why? Why do I

need to know the names and the treasures and the rules? What makes the crown jewels so special, or the place settings so important? Who were all of these kings and queens, anyway?"

Queen Iduna replied, "Well, that is the best part of preparing to be queen. Learning the stories of our people."

"But I don't know any of the stories!" Elsa insisted. "I only know the lists and the rules."

Her mother gave her a patient smile. She unstacked some more plates and placed them on the table in front of her, all in a row. "The stories are in everything we do, Elsa," she said. "Even on these plates. They hold memories of my travels, yes. But also memories that are passed from one generation to the next."

She pointed to the plate Elsa's pancake had been on, now clean. "This crocus is the crest of our kingdom, the symbol of rebirth after a long winter." Elsa had never really thought about the crest before, but she knew the joy of seeing spring's first blossoms.

The next plate showed bright lights in a dark sky, and Queen Iduna said, "The day your papa's parents were married, the

northern lights blazed overhead, just like this. It was a good omen for their reign. This picture shows that bit of history."

Elsa had never heard that detail, but she liked it.

There was a giant white bunny on the next plate, bigger than any Elsa had ever seen. "And here is the mythical snow hare, said to bring good luck to those who can catch him. But he is tricky," the queen said, "so his good luck can be hard to find. Arendelle has many legends like this one."

Elsa studied history every day, but she had never thought of it this way before. It was about facts, yes, but also about stories and legends.

Just then, she heard her father and Anna coming up the path from the village. Her father was walking slowly, scanning the sky for birds. Anna was doing a series of cartwheels. How long had they been gone? The morning had passed quickly after all.

Elsa had wanted to skip her lessons so she could play with her sister and experiment with her magic. But there was another reason, too, one she didn't like to admit.

Sometimes Elsa was nervous about becoming queen. With her power, she knew she'd be unlike any queen Arendelle had ever known, and learning how to use a finger bowl would not make a difference.

But what if her mother's stories would help Elsa understand her place in the kingdom? Those were lessons she could use—and they could last a lifetime.

Chapter 5
Elsa's Mistake

The next few mornings at the Sommerhus followed the same routine as the first. After breakfast, Elsa would join her mother for lessons while Anna and King Agnarr would go play outside.

At the end of every lesson, Queen Iduna would take out one of her special plates and tell Elsa the story that went along with it. The stories almost made Elsa forget about the playtime she was missing with Anna. Almost.

Just as Queen Iduna finished telling Elsa the legend of a horse made of water, Anna burst into the cottage like a tornado. She told Elsa about every animal and flower she'd seen on her walk, barely pausing to catch a breath as she led Elsa upstairs.

Standing in the doorway of the bedroom, Anna narrowed her eyes and looked critically at the fort. "I think we should make it bigger," she told Elsa.

Elsa found extra chairs and blankets in their parents' room. She dragged the chairs to the fort and re-draped the blankets to fit. The new fort was so big that it went beyond their beds and took up almost the girls' entire room!

Anna crouched and went inside. "We need supplies," she said.

"What kind of supplies?" Elsa asked.

Anna thought for a moment. "Art supplies. Some toys. And definitely sweets."

In one corner of the fort, they piled paper and quills in case they wanted to draw pictures. They created a place for toys and books. Anna flopped on her back and announced, "I think we can stay here all summer!"

Hildy and Hanna, their beloved dolls, had a corner of the fort to themselves. Anna made sure each one had a place to sleep, then Elsa remembered a tea set that was buried in the trunk. "Maybe Hildy and Hanna need a place for tea," she said.

Together, the sisters fashioned a table and chairs from a book and two small cushions. But when Elsa uncovered the tea set from the depths of the trunk, she found that the cups and saucers were chipped and coated with dust. Frowning, she told Anna, "Hanna and Hildy deserve better than this. I know something they will like much more."

Elsa hurried downstairs and back to the table, slipping two plates—the crocus and the snow hare—off the top of the stack. Her parents had not seen or heard her take them, since they were walking in the garden.

The family would not need *every* plate at each meal, Elsa told herself as she returned to Anna. Okay, she was not sure she was allowed to play with them. But these plates were special to the whole family, Elsa reasoned. And if the plates were in the fort, she could tell Anna what she had learned about them. Surely, her mother would be okay with that. On top of the plates, Elsa placed a pair of teacups for the dolls.

Back in the fort, Anna had propped Hildy and Hanna in sitting positions on their beds. Elsa gave each doll a teacup and a plate, then a couple of sweets from the kitchen. She swatted away Anna's hand as it snaked toward the treats. "Those are for Hildy and Hanna!" Elsa said.

Anna made a face, but she dropped her hand. Then she poured pretend tea into each cup. Anna acted like she was taking a sip, then blew cool air over the top. "Oh, that's too hot for you," she told the dolls. "You'll need to wait till it cools."

"Or maybe not," said Elsa. She smiled at her sister as an idea came to her. "After all,

I happen to be an expert in ice."

She stretched out her hands. She closed her eyes and concentrated, and when she opened them, there was a misshapen piece of ice resting on each palm. If Elsa squinted hard, they looked like ice cubes that were just the right size for the teacups. She dropped them into the cups as Anna begged, "Again!"

Elsa clamped her eyes shut and thought about ice cubes once more, but something else burst forth in her hands unexpectedly. It was small and lumpy, but she had made a snowball! Elsa held it out for her sister to see.

"Can I touch it?" Anna asked.

"Of course!" Elsa said.

Anna grabbed the snowball and tossed it in the air. She rolled it around in her hands as if she was testing it. Then she got a mischievous glint in her eye, and Elsa could tell what she was thinking. Elsa ducked out of the fort just before Anna could throw the snowball in her direction.

"You can't get me!" Elsa called out. But there was nowhere to hide from Anna, because their little bedroom had been overtaken by the fort.

Elsa ducked into a hallway closet but regretted it. Anna would be waiting for her when she came out, Elsa suspected, and she was right. The moment Elsa peered out of the closet, she felt the snowball splat against her cheek.

Fortunately, she knew how to make another one. *If* her magic behaved as she hoped.

Elsa came out of the closet, acting like their snowball fight was over.

"Let's go back into the fort," she said to her sister. Anna looked at her suspiciously, but Elsa just said, "What?" Anyone could see that her hands were empty.

Anna led the way inside the fort, settling down next to the dolls. Elsa picked up Hildy and gently gave her a sip of pretend tea, which was really a few drops of melted ice. Then, just when Anna was starting to relax into the fort's pillows, Elsa closed her eyes and focused on forming another snow-ball. It took a little more effort, but when she was done she noticed that the snowball she had made was a little firmer, more ice than snow.

"Oh, no you don't!" Anna yelled when she realized what her sister was doing. She grabbed the snowball and lobbed it at Elsa. There was a quick scuffle in the enclosed space of the fort, the sisters batting the snow-ball back and forth like a real ball until it fell from the air with a thud.

Right onto the snow hare plate Elsa had smuggled into the tent.

Breaking it in two.

Chapter 6
The Snow Hare

For Elsa, it felt like time had stopped. She picked up the two pieces of the plate and thought about how it had looked just seconds before. The snow hare had been hopping without a care in the world, and now he was split in half. How had things gone so wrong so fast? The plate was ruined, and it could never be fixed.

Or could it? Could her magic solve this problem? If only she could freeze the pieces back together . . . Elsa tried to use her magic, imagining ice that would connect the two broken sides. But it was as difficult as if she'd never had magic in the first place. Was her power as broken as the plate?

As she stared at the broken plate in her hands, she felt a warm stream of tears pouring down her face. Anna, who noticed Elsa had begun crying, wrapped her arms around her and said, "It's okay. It's going to be okay."

Ignoring Anna's words, Elsa shook

herself free of her sister's embrace and burst out of the fort. Anna meant well, but she didn't understand. The plates were part of the kingdom's history, of the knowledge Elsa was supposed to gain to become queen. How would she ever explain this to her parents?

Elsa wiped away her tears, a look of determination coming over her features. She would have to face the consequences. The sooner she admitted her mistake, the better.

Somehow, she pulled herself together. She changed out of her nightgown and went down the stairs and into the garden. She would own up to what she had done and accept any punishment. She would be as cold as ice.

But her courage melted away as soon as she stepped outside and saw her parents sitting in the shade of an elm tree. "Oh, Mama," she cried, running toward her. "I am so sorry!" She crumpled to the ground by Queen Iduna.

Anna was right behind Elsa, and she explained what had happened. "Elsa borrowed the special plates for a tea party. And then we had a snowball fight . . . and one of them got broken."

King Agnarr's eyes grew wide. "A snowball fight?" he asked.

"I started it with my magic," Elsa said. "It's all my fault! I borrowed the plates, I made the snowballs, and I ruined the snow hare." She still had the pieces of the plate in her hand, and she put them together to show her parents. "He'll never be the same again."

Queen Iduna pulled both of her daughters into her lap. "Shhh . . . shhh." She soothed Elsa, stroking her hair. "Everything will be all right."

"But it won't!" Elsa wailed. "A little piece of the kingdom has been broken. By someone who is supposed to be the queen!" That was the worst part of it all. How could she be entrusted with such a huge responsibility when she couldn't even take care of a plate? Maybe she would *never* be ready to rule a kingdom.

Queen Iduna turned Elsa's face toward her and wiped away her tears. "It will be many years before you are expected to take the throne," she reassured her daughter. "Nobody expects you to be perfect now. You are only learning. And one of the ways we learn is by making mistakes."

Elsa sniffled. She did not like making mistakes, and no matter what her mother said, she knew this was a big one. She took a deep breath. "But now no one will know the legend of the snow hare," she said. She swallowed hard and willed herself not to cry anymore.

"Only the plate is broken," King Agnarr reassured her. "Not the story! The legend is much more important than the plate itself. And it will live in Arendelle forever."

From the other side of the queen's lap, Anna piped up. "What's the legend of the snow hare?"

Queen Iduna leaned back and paused,

as if summoning a precious memory. "The snow hare lives in the woods and fields of Arendelle, blending in with his surroundings all winter long," she said.

"And he is magic?" Anna asked.

Elsa smiled, though her eyes still felt a little puffy. Of course Anna wanted to know about the magic.

"Some say," added the king, "that the snow hare can bring a person good luck for a lifetime."

Anna's eyes widened. "How does he do that?" she asked.

"All you have to do is hold the snow hare in your arms," the queen explained. "But that is easier said than done, because he is almost impossible to catch. He lives in the open, so people may spot him in the woods or fields in summertime. He may even come close, daring us to catch him. In the end, though, the snow hare darts away. He always manages to keep his good luck to himself."

"That's no fair," Anna said. "The snow hare should share his magic with everyone."

But Elsa saw the story differently. Magic could work wonders, but she knew why the snow hare would guard his carefully. Because magic could also be too powerful to control. And when it slipped out of your hands, it could even be a little dangerous.

Chapter 7
The Perfect Summer Night

By the end of their first week at the Sommerhus, the broken plate was just an ache in the back of Elsa's mind, something she could almost forget. She was still in her favorite place with her favorite people, and nothing could ruin that.

One night, near sunset, Anna and Elsa went to the edge of the woods to look for kindling for a fire while Queen Iduna stood nearby. They scampered along the hiking path, piling sticks and pieces of bark into baskets they carried and playing their usual game. "Don't touch the ground!" Elsa said, hopping from root to root. "Anna, you're slipping. . . ." Her sister had one foot on a rock and one on a rickety log.

Anna's gaze was fixed on something deep in the woods. "Shhh," she told her sister, putting a finger to her lips. "I think I see the snow hare!" She pointed into the distance, and Elsa stepped in that direction.

"You touched the ground!" said Anna. "I win this round!"

Elsa frowned. "Were you tricking me?"

she asked. "Did you really see the snow hare at all?"

Anna shook her head. "Okay, I made it up," she admitted. "Because you always win the game."

"I'm older," Elsa said, standing up straight and sticking her chin out.

"And someday you'll be queen," replied Anna, sweeping into a curtsy.

Elsa did not want to think about being queen or imagine what the next day's lessons would bring. In the past few days, she had learned how to write official letters and how to call for the royal guards.

"Don't touch the ground!" she cautioned

her sister, moving up the path and starting the game again. She just wanted to enjoy her time at the Sommerhus, where worries seemed to vanish in the breeze that fanned the fjord.

When their mother led them back to the cottage, King Agnarr was building the fire. He took the kindling from their baskets, feeding the flames until the family's bonfire lit up the early evening. As the sun sank lower in the sky, the fire grew bolder and brighter, crackling with life.

Beside the fire, Anna bounced in anticipation. "When are we roasting marshmallows?"

"Right now!" said Queen Iduna, carrying a bowl full of marshmallows to the fire. Elsa put one on the end of her stick and roasted it patiently. She waited to eat her marshmallow until it was golden brown all around.

Anna, on the other hand, strung five marshmallows along her stick and stuck it into the hottest part of the flames. Soon her marshmallows were black on the outside and raw on the inside, but she didn't care one bit. She tugged them from her stick one by one and devoured them in seconds. As soon as she had finished them, she asked, "Can I have some more?"

"Not tonight," said King Agnarr. His face was lit by the soft glow from the fire. Their father reached down and lifted one of his fiddles to his chin. Keeping time by tapping his toes, the king began to play one of their favorite tunes.

Anna and Elsa sprang up to twirl in circles around the fire, their favorite kind of dancing. And then, when they were tired after a dozen songs, they lay on the grass and watched the twinkling stars.

Elsa imagined connecting the stars to form the shape of a rabbit and thought some more about the snow hare. Why would she need his good luck anyway? Maybe she could use it in the future. Good luck might help her master her magic. Maybe it would even help her when she became the queen. Too bad no one ever caught the snow hare. It was sad he was only a legend.

When the fire died down, it was time for the girls to go to bed. They ducked into their fort and checked on Hildy and Hanna before snuggling into bed. Queen Iduna sat with one arm around each of her daughters as she read them fairy tales; then she tucked them in for the night.

"Sweet dreams," she said. "Tomorrow will be a new adventure!"

The room was dark when their mother left, and shadows moved across the ceiling. Next to Elsa, Anna propped herself up on one elbow. "Want to tell ghost stories?" she asked.

Elsa could already hear the wind howling through the trees. It did sound a little like ghosts, she thought. "Sure!"

She was careful not to make her story too scary for Anna, though. Hers was about a friendly ghost who returned to the same

cottage summer after summer to visit the
place he loved the most.

Anna's story was darker and more dramatic. "This is about the ghosts of the
people who looked for the snow hare but

never found him," she began. "They never found good luck. Actually, all their luck was bad. . . ."

Elsa couldn't let Anna give herself nightmares. "Let's save that one for tomorrow night, okay?" she said. She hugged her sister and closed her eyes, pretending to sleep.

In no time, Anna was breathing evenly, lost to the world of dreams. Elsa wasn't tired yet, but she knew a good way to put herself to sleep. All Elsa needed to do was start reviewing her list of Arendelle's rulers, and she drifted off at once.

In the middle of the night, though, Elsa awoke with a start. For a moment she forgot where she was, but soon she remembered. Their little room, the summer, the fort, the dolls, the plate, the future. But something wasn't right.

Elsa was still half asleep, so it took a moment for her foggy mind to realize what was wrong.

The spot beside her in bed was warm, but her sister wasn't there.

Chapter 8
Chasing Anna

Elsa blinked. Maybe Anna had gone down-stairs for a drink of water or a midnight snack. Maybe she was with their parents, or somewhere else in the Sommerhus.

Elsa wouldn't be able to sleep until she knew, so she rolled out of bed and stretched. Lots of people woke up in the middle of the night, Elsa told herself. Anna's usual way at the Sommerhus was to go to bed late and wake up at the crack of dawn, but that didn't mean she couldn't break her pattern. Maybe nothing was wrong at all.

It was possible. But Elsa had a bad feeling.

She ran her hands along the other side of the bed to make sure her sister wasn't huddled under the blankets. Anna wasn't there.

Elsa slipped out of the room. Should she wake her parents? She did not want them to worry. For now, at least, she decided to search for Anna by herself.

Elsa tiptoed downstairs. The glow of moonlight washed over everything, but the corners were dark and the grandfather clock cast an ominous shadow. Elsa darted into each room, scanning for Anna. "Come out, come out, wherever you are," she whispered, but no one answered.

Would Anna have left the Sommerhus? Most kids wouldn't dare go outside at

night alone, but Elsa knew her sister. Anna was fearless and bold, a girl who wouldn't let anything get between her and her next big idea.

But why? What could Anna want outside? Elsa had no answers, but she knew that Anna shouldn't be alone. She was too little, and it was too dark. Her skin prickled with goose bumps.

Elsa opened the door, taking care not to make any noise, and propped it open with a stone so she could get back in without waking her parents. There was no need to worry them, she decided. Anna couldn't have gone very far.

Stepping outside, Elsa crisscrossed the gardens of the Sommerhus, softly calling, "Anna? Anna? Are you out there?" But there was only silence.

When a cloud drifted over the moon, the grounds around the cottage turned pitch-black. In another section of sky, the stars still winked, so Elsa would have to rely on their dim light to see.

She took a deep breath. Where was she going to go?

Elsa thought again about waking her parents but decided to put it off a little longer. Any minute, she expected to find her sister.

She walked along the
edge of the gardens and
spotted Anna's cloak
near the hiking path.
Had she worn it outside,
then grown too warm? She
had to be close, Elsa thought.

Anna probably wasn't scared, but Elsa
shivered as she hurried along the path.
Wasn't her father always cautioning against
the dangers of the woods? Elsa's imagination ran wild. There could be animals out
there, hungry and fierce. There could even
be monsters. And Elsa knew that a person
could get lost among the trees without

anyone ever realizing they were there.

That was the most frightening thing, Elsa thought—being alone. And thinking of Anna alone, in danger.

Elsa paused for a moment to calm her racing heart, and when she stopped she remembered something: Anna might be alone, but Elsa didn't need to be. Elsa had magic to keep her company.

Her worries made the magic difficult to manage at first. After a few misshapen lumps, though, Elsa finally conjured something that resembled a snowball. Its cold weight in her hands felt reassuring; every time she felt a new surge of worry, she squeezed it to relieve the pressure. Soon the snowball was dented and melting, but Elsa's spirits were restored. Anna couldn't have gone that far, Elsa told herself. Any minute, she would find her.

As she rushed ahead, Elsa's eyes tried to take in every inch of the trail. Strangely, she was getting used to the dark, and as time went on it seemed almost like the forest was allowing her to see things she had never noticed before.

The wind had been howling, but now it tickled Elsa's nose, teasing her like a friend. Leaves rose in a gust, and it looked like they were dancing. Even the taste of the air was sharp and fresh, like lemon or mint. Was this why her mother loved the outdoors so much? Maybe these natural wonders were the true treasures of the kingdom.

Elsa was almost at the top of a hill, which ended at a bluff. She could hear the gentle lapping of water far below. Would Anna have gone down there? Elsa panicked. Could she have been swept out to sea? She squeezed her snowball for comfort, digging her fingernails into its cold center, and then she remembered what Anna had said. The water was too cold. She wouldn't even walk into it. She wouldn't have come this way, Elsa thought. She could feel it in her bones.

She turned around on the trail and headed back the way she had come, relieved to sense Anna wasn't in the water but frustrated that there was still no sign of her sister. If only she had woken her parents at once! She needed help, and she was too far into the forest to turn back. For the hundredth time, Elsa wondered what Anna was thinking. Why was she out there at all?

Elsa was walking near the strawberry bushes, feeling her way past a row of pines, when suddenly she heard a faint voice. Was it the wind? Was it just her imagination?

She wasn't sure until she finally made out the words.

"Elsa, come! I found him! I found the snow hare!"

Chapter 9
A Rescue

Elsa froze in place. It was Anna.

Her voice was louder now. "Elsa! I'm over here!" she said. "I knew you would find me."

Elsa's eyes scanned the forest, but she could barely see beyond the trees in front of her.

"Help me!" Anna called. "I'm stuck!"

Elsa moved toward Anna's voice, keeping

her arms out in front of her so she would not crash into anything. She knew that her sister was nearby, but she wanted to *see* her.

"Help!" Anna cried out again.

Elsa looked up, scanning the treetops, but it was only when she looked down that she understood the problem. She gasped. Only a few steps ahead of her, hidden by shadow and brush, was a deep hole. In the dark, she could barely make out Anna sitting at the bottom.

"I found him, Elsa!" Anna said.

Elsa was confused until she caught sight of her sister's eyes, which were lit with excitement. And her sister's arms, which were full of something white and fluffy, and kicking furiously.

Elsa took a cautious step backward. "What is that?" she asked.

"I told you!" Anna exclaimed. "It's the snow hare!" Now Elsa could see that the white fluff had long ears and a puffy tail. It was larger than any rabbit she had ever seen, but otherwise it looked perfectly normal.

Whether or not it was the legendary bunny, Anna struggled to keep hold of it. "I followed him down here, but now we're stuck. You have to help us out!" she said.

Elsa walked closer to the edge of the hole

and peered down. Someone must have been digging there, maybe to plant or to build something. The hole was deep and wide enough to hold their room in the Sommerhus.

"Oh, Anna . . ." said Elsa. Her sister was asking her to do something that seemed impossible. "The hole is huge!" She didn't want to scare Anna, but she had to be honest. "I don't know how to get you out."

"It's not just me," Anna reminded her, "but also the snow hare. He's coming with me! I saw him outside the cottage from our window and followed him all the way here." She sounded quite proud of herself.

Elsa sighed. She was pretty sure it was

just a regular rabbit. But when Anna got an idea into her head, it was hard to talk her out of it. "Yes, and the snow hare," she agreed. There was no point in fighting about it.

She stretched her arm out to Anna. "I can't reach!" Anna said, extending her own arm as far as it would go. Her fingers grazed Elsa's, but she was too far away to grab it.

"I have a better idea," Elsa said. "I think you have to run and jump to reach my hands."

Anna tried jumping once, and then again, but she lost her footing and landed back at the bottom of the hole. She fell on her back, and the rabbit wiggled free from

her grasp. In a flash, he scrambled up the side of the hole and disappeared into the darkness.

Anna began to cry. "Noooo!" she wailed. "He was supposed to bring us good luck!"

"Shhh, Anna, don't cry," Elsa said, trying to sound calm. "I will get you out of there!" She just had to think for a minute. She sat down at the top of the hole, careful not to fall in herself.

Elsa frowned, feeling hopeless. Someday

a whole kingdom would be hers, but what good would that be if she couldn't even rescue her sister? She didn't have the power to do the one thing she wanted to do the most.

Elsa sat up straight. That was it.

She did have power—the power of her magic.

True, her magic could be trouble, like when it led to her breaking the plate. It could be unpredictable. But when it worked right, it could let her do almost anything.

Maybe even save her sister.

"I'm cold," Anna piped up. "It's dark down here."

Elsa stood and forced herself to sound

cheerful. "Think of it like our fort," she said. "It's your own special hideout! You're perfectly fine in there for now." Elsa did not want Anna to lose hope. She did not want her sister to doubt what she was about to try next.

Anna sniffled and put her head in her hands. "I miss Hildy and Hanna."

"You'll be seeing them in no time," Elsa assured her. If she could get her magic to do exactly what she wanted, that was. It was a big *if*, but she had to try.

Elsa closed her eyes and summoned her power. She would need more than snowballs or icicles. Taking in a deep breath,

Elsa concentrated harder than she ever had before. She'd conjured up a sheet of ice. Could she make stairs? A rope? A slide?

After a few minutes of intense focus, she heard Anna's reaction from below. "Oh!" she said. "I'm skating!" Without realizing it, Elsa had spread a thin layer of ice around the bottom of the hole.

"Sorry!" said Elsa. "Let me try again." That was not quite what she had meant to do. "Anna, can you step off the ice for a second?"

Elsa stared below and concentrated hard.

Stairs would be too difficult, she decided. A rope was too likely to break. But what about a ramp? That meant Elsa had to come up with a sheet of ice that would stretch from the bottom of the hole to the top, where she stood, plus be strong enough to hold Anna. If it broke, Anna would fall.

This was more than Elsa had ever asked of her magic before, and her instinct was to scrunch herself up to control it. Unless . . . would it be better to let her powers go? At once, Elsa knew what to do. She flung her arms out and let magic pour from her fingertips.

She did not dare to look, but Anna told her what she needed to know.

"There's a ramp, Elsa," Anna said with wonder. "Can I walk on it?"

How long would this burst of power last? Elsa finally glanced down at the ramp she was building. It was hard to make out in the dark, but she could see the uneven slope of snow and ice inching to the top of the hole.

"Yes!" Elsa said, once the ramp was long enough for Anna to get out. "But it's very slippery! Please be careful, okay? And hurry! I don't know how long we have."

Elsa's heart felt still as her magic kept

flowing. She was almost frozen with fear, until she saw Anna emerge from the hole. Her sister was fine, and it didn't matter that the magic was beginning to fade. Elsa was brave, and Anna was safe; and if they were really lucky, they could get back to the Sommerhus before sunrise.

Chapter 10
A New Day

The first hints of dawn spread across the sky as the sisters walked back home. Anna was unusually quiet, and Elsa was lost in thought. How would they explain to their parents what had happened? Even if they might get in trouble, Elsa wanted her mom and dad to know how she had used her magic to help Anna. It was a good sign for the future, she thought. Maybe someday she'd have full control over her power!

Control over her little sister was another story, she thought. Turning to Anna, Elsa said, "What were you thinking, sneaking out like that? Something terrible could have happened."

"Something terrible *did* happen," Anna pointed out. "But you saved me, just like I knew you would."

Elsa had to smile. Her sister had so much faith in her.

"I woke up in the middle of the night," Anna explained, "and I was thinking about our ghost stories. And then, from the window, I could see a bunny. I knew it was the snow hare! I just had to chase him. What if I never got another chance to catch his good luck?"

"What do you need good luck for?" Elsa asked.

"No, no, it wasn't for me," explained Anna. "The good luck was supposed to be for you."

"For me?" Elsa asked. She looked at Anna in surprise. She didn't understand.

"To help you when you become queen," Anna said. "I thought you could use a little extra luck. Just in case."

Elsa's heart warmed. She didn't need good luck when she had a sister like Anna. Her sister might be the kindest girl in the whole world, she thought.

"I'm sorry you lost the snow hare," Elsa said, hugging Anna.

"It's okay," replied Anna. "I'll find him again someday, I just know it."

Did her sister even understand the difference between real life and legends? There was no such thing as a snow hare, or at least not one that could change your life forever. But there was no convincing Anna, so Elsa just smiled and said, "I hope you do."

When they reached the Sommerhus, they tugged open the door and listened carefully. They couldn't hear their parents at all. They were still in bed!

"Let's make them breakfast!" Anna said.

But her idea of breakfast was more like dessert. Elsa didn't have the heart to tell her that no one else would want to eat a bowl of strawberries stuck together with syrup and chocolate.

Elsa set the table with her mother's

special plates and sat down with her parents after they had come downstairs rubbing their eyes.

"What is this?" asked King Agnarr. "A party?"

Elsa and Anna nodded. Before Elsa could explain why they were awake so early, Anna beat her to it.

"We went on an adventure!" her little sister exclaimed.

The king and queen were not happy to hear of their daughters' nighttime outing.

"The forest can be dangerous," King Agnarr pointed out, as he had many times before. "Anything could have happened, and we would never have known where to look for you."

But the king and queen were happy to eat the strawberries—or they acted happy, anyway—and happy to hear that Elsa's magic had saved Anna from the hole in the woods.

"The magic did exactly what you asked?" said Queen Iduna. She put an arm around Elsa and hugged her. "I'm so proud of you!"

Those words were music to Elsa's ears, and after hearing them she did not even mind washing the dishes. For the next few days, their parents said, the girls would be doing some extra work around the cottage to make up for leaving the house without permission in the middle of the night.

Soon it was time for Elsa to go back to her lessons. She got a lump in her throat when Anna left to play outside and she was stuck studying an old book about Arendelle's best-known artists and musicians. It took Elsa a while to settle into it, but after she did, she saw what made those people special. They might not have had magic, but they were clever and resourceful, bold and courageous.

"You did a brave thing, helping your sister," Queen Iduna said as Elsa finished

the last chapter of her book. She leaned over

and put a hand on Elsa's shoulder, giving it

a gentle squeeze. "You are going to make a

great leader someday."

Elsa smiled at her mom, the queen's words filling her with warmth. She had always worried her magic would make it harder to be a good queen, but maybe her power didn't make her so different from the rulers of the past after all.

"I think you've read enough for today," said Queen Iduna "You're free to go and play with Anna."

Elsa put down her book and raced outside to look for Anna, but there was no sign of her sister. Not again!

"Have you seen Anna anywhere?" she asked her father.

King Agnarr looked up from the book he was reading, and said, "I just saw her, but I think she must have gone inside."

Taking the stairs two at a time, Elsa ran to their room and pushed open the door. When she didn't spot Anna, she knew her sister had to be in the fort.

"Hello, girls," she said to Hildy and Hanna, who were by the window. Then she peeked inside the fort. "Anna?" she said. It was strangely quiet in there.

"Shhh," Anna whispered. "He's sleeping."

Elsa wasn't sure if it was lucky or unlucky, but her sister never gave up on anything. She

must have been searching all morning, Elsa realized, but she'd finally found what she wanted.

Curled up on Anna's lap was a large white rabbit. "The rest of our summer will be perfect," she predicted with a grin. "Because I finally caught the snow hare."

DISNEY
Before the Story

Tiana's
BEST SURPRISE

By
TESSA ROEHL

ILLUSTRATED BY
ARIANNA REA

Chapter 1
A Delicious Dream

Tiana's eyes opened wide. It had only been a dream. But it felt so real, she could still smell it: the spices, the bubbling broth, and all the love stirred into the gumbo. She could see it, too: Happy faces sharing the meal, her daddy happiest of all. Enjoying gumbo so perfect it sparkled. The *best* gumbo ever.

It was early. Earlier than the time her mama usually popped her head in and said,

"Tiana, up and at 'em. The stars have gone to bed, and it's your turn to shine now." The sun was just starting to peek through her window. But it wasn't the morning light that had woken her. It was her dream and the plan that had started forming in her head.

Tiana threw off her covers, got dressed, made her bed, and darted out of her room. There wasn't a drop of sleep left in her now.

She burst into the kitchen, ready to tell her mama all about the dream and the plan. But the sight of her daddy at the stove closed her mouth up tight before the words could tumble out. She ran to his side, wrapping her arms around his waist.

He smiled down at her, that smile where his mouth stretched wide and his eyes crinkled, making her feel as warm as the heat rising from the stove. Tiana almost never got the chance to see him off to work. He left too early, when the sky was still dark. "Perfect timing," he said. "I'm making the *best* scrambled eggs ever."

"The best?" Tiana asked.

"That's what he keeps saying." Tiana's mama laughed. She was seated at the kitchen table.

"Well," her daddy said, frowning, "they *will* be the best scrambled eggs ever . . . once Tiana tells me what they're missing."

Tiana grinned. She took the bite he was holding out for her to taste.

"Now, don't you say hot sauce, because that's already in there," he said.

"I *know,* Daddy. I can taste it," Tiana said. "Hmmm." She closed her eyes, focusing on the flavors on her tongue. Salt, pepper, onion, parsley . . . *Aha!* "Bell peppers!" she cried.

"Bell peppers, you say?" Her daddy reached into the vegetable bin.

Tiana nodded. "They'll add just the right crunch."

He handed Tiana a red bell pepper and watched her make careful cuts. "Eudora,

I've taught this girl well in her eight years, haven't I?"

"You sure have, James," her mama said. "Taught her nose to wake her up for a good breakfast. Is that what got you rushing down here so early, Tiana?"

Tiana avoided looking at her mother and focused on scooping the peppers into the eggs. Her daddy handed her the spoon to continue stirring as he fetched plates from the cupboard. The dream she'd had about *the best gumbo ever* was still right there in her head. But she couldn't say anything about it yet. Part of what was going to make it the best ever was that it would be a surprise. "I've got to start waking up early, Mama. Practice for our restaurant."

"Tiana's Place," her daddy said, winking at her as he took the spoon back and served up the eggs.

"Tiana's Place," Tiana agreed, helping him carry the plates to the table.

"Tiana's Place," her mama chimed in as she began eating. "Once New Orleans gets a taste of your daddy's gumbo, folks will be lining up for blocks. You'll have to wake up well before the sun to prepare for all those customers."

Tiana blew on her eggs to cool them down. "I won't sleep ever again if it means

Daddy and I can have our restaurant." Her daddy had been working so much lately, she barely got to see him anymore. She knew it was good for their savings, which her daddy kept in coffee cans that he stuffed with his extra bills and coins. The cans were getting fuller and fuller. Someday soon, they'd be able to afford Tiana's Place. But she wanted him to take a break and have someone do something nice for him for once. That was where her plan came in.

Her daddy stood up, his plate empty. Her mama handed him his lunch pail. "Hard work is going to get us that restaurant, and that's what I'm off to do." He kissed Tiana on the top of her head. "Sleep is pretty important, too, though. Two more days and then it's Sunday and I'll have the whole evening free." He  looked over his shoulder as he opened the door. "Maybe we can make something for dinner? What do you say, Tiana?"

"No!" Tiana nearly spit out her eggs as she yelled. Her father looked confused. "I mean . . . Sunday's your birthday. You shouldn't have to work on your birthday," she finished, shooting a glance at her mother for help.

Her mama laughed. "We've got your birthday plans covered." Her daddy ruffled Tiana's hair, and then he was gone.

Tiana's mother gave her a knowing look. "What's cooking in that head of yours?"

"Mama, I had the most delicious dream." Tiana set her fork down and pushed her plate away.

"Delicious?" her mama asked. She pointed back at Tiana's plate, her eyes telling Tiana she'd better eat up.

Tiana took two more bites. "I saw it, Mama. In my dream. *I* made the *best* gumbo ever."

"You and your daddy already make the

best gumbo ever.
Everyone on this
block knows so."
Her mama pointed at the
plate again.

"But this time I made it all by myself. No help from Daddy—just his gumbo pot, of course." Tiana took another bite before her mama could give her that look again. "It was so perfect it sparkled! And everyone from the neighborhood was there to taste it, and . . . oh, Mama, best of all: we surprised Daddy! I've never seen him so happy."

"That is a lovely dream, baby."

Tiana swallowed the last bite and took

the breakfast plates to the sink to wash. "I'm going to make it real," she said. "Since Sunday is Daddy's birthday, we'll invite everyone over for a party, only he won't know about it. And he won't know I've already made the gumbo. All he'll have to do is show up! It'll be perfect."

Her mama joined her at the sink to help dry the dishes. "I agree. If you're in charge, it will be perfect."

Tiana smiled. "Oh, and Big Daddy and Charlotte will come, of course."

"Of course." Her mama nodded. "Seeing as how Sunday is the day after tomorrow, I think we'd better go tell the neighbors your plan, don't you?"

"Yes!" Tiana was thrilled. Her dream was going to come true.

Chapter 2
The New Neighbor

An hour later, when the neighborhood began to stir, Tiana and her mama set out to visit their neighbors before everyone left for school, work, or errands. Tiana skipped off the porch and grabbed her mom's hand, tugging her across the street to the Johnsons' house. Marnie Johnson, who everyone called Grandma Marnie, was already outside in her rocking chair.

"Good morning, Tiana, dear. Morning, Eudora."

"Grandma Marnie!" Tiana called. Her mama squeezed her hand. "Oh, I mean, good morning," she said. "We're having a party for my daddy on Sunday. At five p.m. It's a surprise!"

Grandma Marnie nodded, still rocking away. "You know I'll be there. Gumbo?"

"Gumbo," Tiana said. "I'm going to make it all by myself."

"If it's half as good as your daddy's, be sure you make extra."

Her mother waved good-bye. "Give my best to the family, Marnie."

"And tell all the Johnsons to come," Tiana added.

"Oh, but if they come, that's less gumbo for me." Grandma Marnie chuckled.

Tiana continued to the house next door, her mama close behind. Little Emile Monroe opened the door just a crack, peeking out at Tiana, his eyes wide. He quickly slammed it shut.

"Sugar, can you go fetch your mama for us?" Tiana's

mother called through the door. Footsteps sounded from inside.

"Why is he so afraid of me and not of you? I'm closer to his age!" Tiana exclaimed. She never understood why Emile always hid from her.

Her mama laughed. "Sometimes a little sugar goes farther than spice, Tiana."

Tiana shook her head. That didn't make any sense.

Moments later, Emile's mama, Annette Monroe, came to the door.

"Look at you two, out and about so early." Annette grinned. Tiana had always liked Annette. Something in her eyes made Tiana feel as if she knew how to have fun. As if she would definitely throw a fantastic surprise party.

"Tiana has something she'd like to ask you," her mom said.

"We're having a surprise party for my daddy on Sunday evening. I'll be making gumbo, and all the Monroes are expected to be there," Tiana said.

"Are we, now?" Annette laughed. Emile was peeking out from behind her. Tiana frowned at him, and he darted back behind his mother's skirt. "Well, in that case, we'll be there. Your dad is lucky to have such a thoughtful daughter."

Tiana hopped off the porch. "See you Sunday! Five o'clock! Bye, Emile!" As she waved, Emile ran out of sight.

Tiana and her mom continued down the block. They stopped at the Dupres', the Potters', the Keans', the Gilmores', the Rices', and finally, the Wildes'. After Mr. Wilde quizzed Tiana on her gumbo recipe and she answered his questions to his satisfaction, she was ready to go home and get planning. She started to head back, when her mom stopped her.

"Tiana, we haven't reached the end of the block," her mama said.

"We've called on everyone, Mama."

"Not everyone." Her mama pointed at the next house, the last one on the street. Tiana had never visited the house before. As far as she knew, no one lived there. The houses on her block weren't grand. They weren't anything like the house where Big Daddy and Charlotte lived. They were smaller, not filled with fancy furniture, elegant drapes, or shiny silver. They were stuffed tight with family, food, and a few possessions. And, of course, love. But the house her mama was pointing at looked older and smaller than the others

on the block. Was the inside going to be like the rest of the houses she knew? Or would it be different?

Her mama took her by the hand again. "Nothing to worry about, Tiana. Just someone new for you to meet."

"Someone new?" Tiana wasn't sure how to feel about someone new. She hadn't seen any *new* faces in her dream.

"Mrs. Isabel Marquez. She just moved in last month. We should include everyone and welcome her to the neighborhood. That's what your daddy would do, isn't it?" Her mama gazed down at her.

Tiana's daddy always said that what he

loved about food was how it brought people together. All people. Tiana nodded and let her mother lead her toward the house. Besides, she thought, someone new to taste her gumbo—that was surely a good thing. She quickened her pace and even felt a little excited when her mom knocked on the door.

An older woman opened it. She was older than Tiana's mama for sure, though not quite as old as Grandma Marnie. Her gray hair was gathered in a bun. Her face was serious, but her skin looked soft. "Good morning," the woman said. The way she spoke sounded different from the way Tiana and her mama spoke. Tiana had heard lots of different accents around New Orleans: French, Creole, German, Irish, Italian, and more. But she wasn't sure what this accent was.

"Good morning," Tiana said.

"Mrs. Marquez, you may remember me from when I came by just after you moved in. I'm Eudora. This is my daughter, Tiana. She has something to ask you." Tiana's mama squeezed her hand. She was always sending messages with those squeezes.

Tiana gulped, feeling shyer than she

had in a long while and wanting to hide behind her mother's skirts, like Emile. But the gumbo and her daddy's surprise were more important. "We're having a party on Sunday night at five o'clock. For my daddy. It's a surprise. We'd—I'd like you to come. I'm making gumbo."

"Gumbo?" Mrs. Marquez asked.

"Have you tasted New Orleans gumbo yet?" Tiana asked. "I promise you'll like it. No one on earth can taste it and not like it."

Mrs. Marquez smiled. Or at least, Tiana thought it was a smile. She wasn't sure. Something about this woman seemed nervous, too, as if she might want skirts of her own to hide behind. "*Sí.* Yes. Gumbo. I would like that very much." She nodded at Tiana. "Thank you, Tiana. Thank you, Eudora." Mrs. Marquez rolled the *r* in *Eudora.* Tiana liked it. It sounded like . . . yes, that was it—Spanish.

"Looking forward to seeing you then," Tiana's mom said. And with that, Tiana and her mother headed home.

"That wasn't so bad, was it?" her mama asked.

Tiana shook her head. "Not so bad at all. Can we go shopping for ingredients now?"

"Now? It's Friday," her mama said as they walked back inside their house. "You've got to get off to school soon, and I've got a dress to finish up for Charlotte. But tomorrow, when I deliver it, you can come along. We'll stop by the big market in town afterward. Deal?"

A visit to her best friend, and a chance to shop at the big city market? "Deal!" Tiana exclaimed.

Chapter 3
Charlotte's Idea

The next day, Tiana and her mother took the streetcar to Charlotte and Big Daddy's house. As they walked through the garden toward the big double doors of the mansion, a cloud of pink and yellow ran through the neatly trimmed trees. Charlotte was racing toward them, followed by her puppy, Stella, and her cat, Marcel.

"Tiana, Tiana, Tiana!" Charlotte threw

her arms around Tiana, almost knocking her over. Charlotte's big blue eyes were nearly hidden by the blond curls that had fallen into her face. "I didn't know you were coming today!"

Stella yipped, circling everyone's ankles. Marcel hung back, eyeing the action. He had a habit of getting trampled when Charlotte got excited.

"We just planned it yesterday. I have a surprise to tell you about!" Tiana said.

Charlotte clasped her hands to her mouth and squealed. "A surprise? Oh, oh, tell me, tell me!"

But before Tiana could say anything, her

mama took both girls gently by the shoulders and steered them toward the big double doors. "Let's talk surprises as we get this dress fitted."

Charlotte skipped up the front steps to her house. "A surprise *and* a new dress? What a day!"

In Charlotte's room, Tiana sat on the plush carpet under the large window that looked out onto the back gardens. Charlotte was in the middle of the room, covered in lace, ribbon, and taffeta. She was squirming and wriggling as Tiana's mom sewed a delicate row of beads along the dress collar.

"Charlotte, dear. I don't think you would like it much if you bumped into this needle." Tiana's mama was being very patient.

Charlotte clenched her fists and stood still. "If Tiana would just tell me her surprise already, I might be able to calm down."

Stella crawled into Tiana's lap. Tiana responded by giving her a belly rub. "I'm throwing a surprise party for my dad. Tomorrow night. You and Big Daddy are invited!"

Charlotte's eyes grew wide. She jiggled her feet and leapt toward Tiana. Tiana's mama held her in place, clutching the ribbon around her shoulder. Charlotte took a step back. "A surprise party?"

Tiana nodded. "Yes! I was inspired by a dream I had."

"A dream?" Charlotte squealed.

"Yup!" Tiana said. She knew Charlotte would love that part. "And in my dream, I made the *best* gumbo ever. Mama and I are going to the market later to buy all the ingredients."

"Oh, my!" Charlotte was about to burst out of her dress with excitement. "I love a good party. And a good surprise! You must let me help."

"Do you want to come over and help me cook?" Tiana asked.

Charlotte nodded as she scooped Marcel into her arms, running her hands through his white fur. "I want to help you with *everything*! We can go to the market together, we can cook together, we can do it all."

Charlotte turned to Tiana's mother. "Miss Eudora, could Big Daddy and I please take Tiana to the market? Then she could stay the night and we could cook the gumbo here."

"Oh, please, Mama," Tiana chimed in. But then a thought struck her. "If I cook here, I won't have my daddy's gumbo pot. . . ."

"We have every kind of pot you could imagine. And besides," Charlotte continued, "if you're cooking in your own kitchen, how will you keep the gumbo a secret from your dad?"

"That's true," Tiana said. She hadn't considered that. Her daddy would know what was happening the minute he got home. "Mama?" Tiana looked up at her mother.

"As long as Big Daddy says it's okay, it's okay with me," her mama said.

"EEEEEE!" Charlotte squealed. Marcel flew out of her arms and ran from the room. Charlotte clasped Tiana's hands and the two friends danced up and down. "This is going to be the greatest surprise party ever!"

Chapter 4
The French Market

Getting Big Daddy to agree to Charlotte and Tiana's plan was as easy as Charlotte saying please. He could never say no to his daughter. So Charlotte changed out of her new dress, Tiana's mama left for home, and the girls headed out the door with Big Daddy for the French Market.

Tiana had been to some of the markets in New Orleans before, but not the French

Market. It was bigger, grander, noisier, and more exciting than anything she had ever seen. Everywhere she looked there was someone shouting, selling, buying, sampling, laughing, bargaining, or arguing. People were bustling back and forth, purchasing the freshest ingredients for their weekend suppers. The air was filled with the scent of fresh seafood, steaming hot bread, strange spices, and sweet sugary somethings. Tiana's eyes were as big as saucers—*this* was where she wanted to be. Maybe one day, she'd come back with her daddy to buy ingredients for Tiana's Place.

Charlotte and Tiana stayed close to Big Daddy, who, dressed in his finest Saturday suit, was the perfect person to head into a crowd with. Not only was he tall, he was also important. He ran the biggest sugar company in Louisiana, so he was no stranger to the market. Everyone seemed to know who he was and made way for him and the girls.

"Where should we go first, Tiana?" Charlotte asked.

"These are the ingredients I need." Tiana set down her shopping basket and showed Charlotte the recipe she had written out the night before. "What my daddy always uses. His special blend of salt, pepper, cayenne, thyme, and oregano. Flour and butter for the roux—"

"The what? The roo?" Charlotte scrunched her nose.

"Roux. It's French. Fat and flour together. It's the most important part, the base of the whole gumbo!" Tiana continued scanning her recipe. "The holy vegetable trinity: celery, bell peppers, and onions. Sausage, hot sauce—without a doubt—and if I can drive a *hard bargain* like my daddy always does"—Tiana clutched a small coin purse in her hand—"I'll have enough left for crab." The night before, she'd emptied out her own coffee-can savings—all the money she'd made from helping her mama out with seamstress jobs.

"Then crab you shall have!" Charlotte shouted.

"We have to drive a hard bargain, though, Lottie. Daddy says that's the most important thing to remember at the market."

"What's a bargain?" Charlotte asked.

Tiana laughed, hoisting up her basket. "Come on." But as they took another step into the market, they realized Big Daddy's path was taking a sharp left—toward a stall selling fresh beignets.

Oil sizzled in a giant pot over an open fire behind the stall. From the pot, the beignet maker removed hot lumps of fried dough with a pair of tongs. He tossed the beignets onto a big platter, coated them with powdered sugar, and laid them out for display. Tiana couldn't blame Big Daddy for following the smell—it was enough to make anyone's mouth water. She could never eat just one when she made them with her dad. But beignets were not what she had come to the market for.

"Big Daddy!" Charlotte had noticed her father's distraction as well.

"Oh, uh . . ." Big Daddy looked at the girls, then back at the tray. "I just need to, eh, do some business over here for a moment.

Make sure this sugar tastes okay. Go ahead with your shopping. Stay in this aisle and I'll catch up to you." Big Daddy turned back to the beignets and started grabbing them by the handful.

"Let's see what's up this way," Charlotte said, pulling Tiana deeper into the market.

They passed stalls selling all sorts of things Tiana had never seen before: exotic-looking fruits, smelly cheeses, unusual spices. One stall was even selling *frogs' legs,* of all things.

"Gross!" Tiana said as they walked by.

"Frogs' legs are a delicacy. Don't you know that?" Charlotte asked.

Tiana shook her head. "Uh-uh, Lottie. I don't like frogs alive, and I *certainly* don't like them . . . not alive."

They soon had everything Tiana needed. She found butter and flour, making an excellent deal on both. She found vegetables and spices at a reasonable price. She even found a lovely link of smoked pork sausage, which she got for a steal by pretending to walk away until the vendor lowered his price. She bought a small bottle of hot sauce from a woman who made it from a family recipe. When she heard that Tiana was making gumbo for her daddy, the kind woman sold it to her for half price.

Finally, Tiana and Charlotte reached the stall selling the last ingredient on Tiana's list. She'd done so well at stretching every penny and charming the vendors that she had enough money left for at least one crab leg . . . maybe two.

"Last ingredient, Tiana," Charlotte said as they admired the display of fresh crab.

Tiana pictured her daddy's face glowing with happiness just as it had in her dream. "It's going to be the *best* gumbo ever."

She was just about to call the crab vendor over when she heard someone say "Pssst" behind her. "You want to make the best gumbo ever?" the voice said. "That won't make it the best. But I have something that will."

Tiana and Charlotte spun on their heels to see who was speaking to them. There stood a boy no older than they were. He was wearing a shirt and slacks that were nicer than anything anyone else was wearing in the market, except perhaps Big Daddy.

A worn gray beret sat atop his head.

Tiana frowned at him. "I know exactly how to make the best gumbo ever. And what I need to do it."

The boy shrugged, turning away. "If you say so," he said, strolling toward a stall at the end of the aisle. There were no products on display that Tiana could see from where she was standing. The only thing that stood out about the stall were the beads wrapped around the wooden posts.

Charlotte gripped Tiana's shoulders. "He's so handsome, don't you think?"

"Handsome?" Tiana made a face. "What does handsome have to do with anything?"

"Princes in fairy tales are always handsome," Charlotte said with a dreamy expression on her face. She glanced in the direction of the stall the boy had disappeared into.

Tiana snorted. "A prince? In the French Market? A fairy tale? Ha!"

"What?" Charlotte cried. "I've seen him at the market before. Maybe he's not a prince, but he could be someone special." She batted her eyelashes at Tiana. "What's the harm in taking a look at what he's selling?"

Tiana let out a sigh. Charlotte had been

helping her all day. She supposed she could return the favor. "Okay. We'll take a look—quickly!" she warned.

That was all it took to set Charlotte skipping off toward the mysterious stall. Tiana looked longingly at the crab legs before following her.

Chapter 5
A Magic Ingredient

iana stepped into the stall. Charlotte was running her fingers over the multicolored beads decorating the posts. It was completely empty inside except for a bookcase filled with bottles of strange-looking sauces. The boy was standing next to the case, waiting.

"*This* is what's going to make my gumbo the best ever?" Tiana asked the boy doubtfully. He just smirked and nodded toward the bottles.

She picked up one of the bottles to examine the liquid inside. It looked like green sauce. She shook the bottle gently. It sloshed around like . . . green sauce. She opened the cap and smelled it. It smelled like nothing. She returned the bottle to the shelf.

"That doesn't look like any gumbo ingredient I've ever seen," Tiana said, folding her arms.

The boy smirked again. "That's because it's not a gumbo ingredient. It's a *magic* ingredient."

"Magic?" Tiana frowned.

"Magic?!" That got Charlotte's attention. She darted away from the beads and grabbed one of the bottles.

"Magic sauce," the boy added.

"I already have hot sauce," Tiana said.

The boy shook his head. "Not hot. Not cold. Not sweet. Not mild. *Magic.* Guaranteed

to make anything you add it to taste the *best* it can possibly taste."

The boy's words had a smoothness to them, almost as if he were singing. His description came just a little too easily and a little too quickly. But the word *best* stuck in Tiana's ear.

"Oh, Tiana," Charlotte said, turning the bottle over in her hands. "A magic ingredient? You have to buy it. You have to! Have to! Have to!"

Tiana tried to keep her head straight. She'd set out to the market with a plan and a list of ingredients. She'd known exactly what she was doing, and now . . . "I still have to buy crab. I don't have money for anything extra."

The boy chuckled. "With this magic sauce, you won't need crab. Your gumbo will taste like there's crab inside. In fact"—he smiled at Charlotte and she blushed—"it will taste like the whole ocean. Like there's shrimp, fish, crab, even *lobster* in that gumbo of yours."

"Lobster!" Charlotte cried.

Tiana shook her head. "One ingredient does all that? Sounds a lot like a shortcut. Taking the easy way. And that's not the way to make gumbo. That's not the way to do anything. At least, it's not the way my mama and daddy taught me."

The boy met Tiana's eyes. "Isn't the easy way doing what you already know?"

Tiana had never thought about it like that. "Well, I ought to at least *taste* this magic sauce."

"You can taste it," the boy said. "But if you taste it now, the magic will be gone by the time you put it in your gumbo."

"Gone? What kind of nonsense is that?" Tiana asked.

The boy shrugged. "That's just the way it works. It uses up its magic on whatever you

add it to. You want to waste that on a taste now, go ahead. But you taste it, you buy it."

Tiana cocked her head, thinking. The boy continued. "You can't really make the *best* gumbo ever if it isn't any different from what you've made before."

Best. There was that word again. It tugged at the dream still playing in her mind. She had pictured herself making gumbo the way she knew how, just like her daddy did. But the boy was right. How could it be the best if it was the same as it always was? Her dad deserved the *best.*

And then Tiana noticed something about the bottle in Charlotte's hands. A ray of sunlight bounced off the glass, and the green sauce sparkled in the light.

The gumbo in her dream had sparkled, too.

Tiana pulled her last coins from her purse and handed them to the boy. He nodded at her. Charlotte handed Tiana the bottle, beaming at her decision.

They left the stall and headed back down the aisle. Big Daddy was up ahead. It looked as if he'd moved on to sampling the sugar at the pie stand. Tiana tucked the bottle of magic sauce in her basket, hoping she was one step closer to the gumbo she'd seen in her dream.

Chapter 6
Chop, Mix, Stir

*W*hoosh. The stove fire blazed to life under the large pot.

"Thank you, Miss Emily," Tiana said to the cook. Big Daddy had insisted that Emily, the LaBouff family cook, start the fire on the stove and stay close by while the girls were in the kitchen.

"You sure you don't want help, Tiana?"

Miss Emily asked, eyeing Tiana's overflowing market basket.

"No, thank you. I'm going to make this gumbo myself from beginning to end," Tiana said with confidence.

"She won't even let *me* help, Miss Emily." Charlotte pouted.

"You girls just holler if you need anything." Miss Emily left the kitchen and Charlotte sat down on the floor to play with her pets.

Tiana was ready to begin. She looked at all the ingredients before her and got that happy stomach flip she always did before

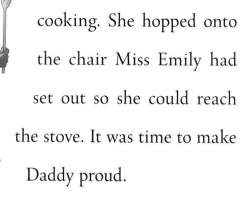

cooking. She hopped onto the chair Miss Emily had set out so she could reach the stove. It was time to make Daddy proud.

The first step in making gumbo was the roux. She couldn't ruin it—she had just enough ingredients for one try. Tiana unwrapped the butter from the paper and dropped it into the pot, watching it sizzle and sputter. She added the flour bit by bit, stirring hard as she went. *Never stop stirring,* her daddy's voice rang in her head. The paste darkened from white to the color of rich caramel. *If you keep stirring, the roux will brown up so thick and rich and nice, that gumbo won't stand a chance to be anything but the best thing you've ever tasted. Stir, stir, stir. Add more flour. Stir, stir, stir.* When the roux reached the color of milk chocolate, she knew it was ready.

Tiana turned her attention to the next stage: the holy trinity of veggies she'd already chopped under Miss Emily's supervision. Into the pot they went. Then it was the sausage's turn, soaking up that veggie flavor and adding its smoky taste. Next came the broth she'd been simmering in another pot with all the spices.

It was fun doing this all by herself. With each ingredient, the aroma in the kitchen grew, letting Tiana know that the flavor was building just right. It smelled so good that Stella wandered away from Charlotte and sat at the bottom of Tiana's stool, hoping to catch any drops that might fall. Tiana didn't blame her. She finally snuck a spoonful herself, and . . . *Mmmm!* If it didn't taste just as good as her daddy's gumbo! Not *quite* the best yet, though.

It was time to add the magic ingredient.

Tiana picked up the bottle. She saw the sparkle again as the light from the stove fire reflected off of it. "Here goes nothing," she

said as she poured a few drops of magic into the gumbo.

She stirred and watched, waiting. For what, she wasn't sure. Fireworks? Something magical to happen? She took a small sip. The gumbo tasted just the same.

Tiana added more sauce. Considering it was magic, she figured the more the better. As she stirred, she noticed that the mixture was thickening. Something *was* happening after all! She added more magic sauce. The gumbo was getting harder to stir. Nervous, Tiana added even more, hoping it would turn the stew into something *magical* soon . . . but her gumbo was quickly turning into something more like glue! The wooden spoon was sticking straight up from the pot, as if it were stuck in a vat of gooey swamp mud.

"Uh-oh," Tiana said. She scrambled off the stool and filled a pitcher with water, hoping she could thin the stew out. She raced back over to the stove and poured the water in, trying to get it back to the tasty soup it had been just moments before. But when Tiana added the water, something very strange happened. The gumbo started frothing, roiling, bubbling up, up, *up* the sides of the pot.

"Uh-oh!" Tiana yelled. Charlotte raced over just in time to see the top of the gumbo slosh over the sides of the pot and spill onto the floor.

"Uh-oh!" Charlotte echoed.

Tiana dove out of the way and hid behind the counter, Charlotte, Marcel, and Stella on her heels. They watched, wincing, as the stew continued to pour onto the floor like a gumbo volcano.

After what felt like forever, the pot finally stopped spitting out gumbo. Tiana approached the stove. She nudged at the remaining gumbo with the spoon. It wasn't gumbo anymore. It was some kind of dark sludge, thick and stiff. She wasn't sure she'd even be able to get the spoon out.

This was not the best gumbo ever. This was the *worst* gumbo ever. Tiana's dream vanished in front of her eyes.

Chapter 7
Not So Magic After All

Tiana slumped down on the floor and let her tears fall. Stella trotted over to her and licked the salty tears streaming down her cheeks. Charlotte knelt and placed a hand on her friend's shoulder.

"Do you want to start again?" she asked softly. "You were doing so well."

Tiana shook her head, tears flowing.

"I only had enough money for the ingredients I already bought. They're gone now. I ruined the gumbo."

"But we have some of those ingredients here. And Big Daddy could take us to buy the rest in the morning," Charlotte said.

Charlotte and Big Daddy were always generous with their good fortune. But it didn't feel right to take from their pantries. *Everything* felt wrong now. Tiana wouldn't be using the ingredients she'd earned. And even though the magic sauce was silly and clearly not magic at all, she couldn't shake the feeling the boy had put in her head. The same gumbo she'd always made with her daddy wasn't going to be any different. It wasn't going to be the *best*.

"I failed, Lottie. Maybe I wasn't meant to make the best gumbo ever. Maybe the dream I had was just that . . . a dream, meant to stay in my head at night and not come into the day." Tiana sniffled.

"I was sure magic was going to be the key," Charlotte said as she sat down next to Tiana.

"I tried to take the easy way . . . and that was wrong." Tiana scratched Stella's ear, thanking her for drying her tears. "I'd better get to cleaning. This mess isn't pretty." Tiana

fetched a rag and bucket from the broom
closet.

"I'll help," Charlotte said.

"You're going to clean?" Tiana asked,
surprised.

"Oh—I meant I was going to ask Miss
Emily or the maid to come in and do it."
Charlotte looked at the cleaning supplies
in Tiana's hands, realizing that her friend

had something different in mind. "But you're right. No more easy way tonight!"

Charlotte grabbed a rag and, after studying the way Tiana scrubbed the floor with soap and water, began to help. The girls wiped up the gumbo sludge from the stove, the floor, and the pot. When the LaBouffs' kitchen was finally back to normal, over an hour had passed, and the girls were exhausted. Charlotte took the rag out of Tiana's hands and led her upstairs, a friendly hand on her shoulder.

A short while later, Tiana was tucked into a cot between Charlotte's bed and the great big window that looked out onto the starry sky.

Charlotte's whisper broke the silence. "How about that evening star, Tiana?" she said. "Wish on it. Wish, wish, wish and things will work out tomorrow."

Tiana sighed. "If only a wish were enough, Lottie. That star can't make gumbo better than I can." She paused. "Well, actually . . . maybe it can."

Charlotte sighed in return, and Tiana heard her nestle deeper under her covers. "Good night, Tiana."

"Good night, Lottie." But Tiana kept her eyes fixed on the evening star. It almost seemed to wink at her, begging her to try her luck on a silly magical thing for the second time that day. *Okay, Star,* Tiana thought. *If there's any magic in the world—even just a sparkle—maybe you could find a way to send some of it to me tomorrow.*

And then she closed her eyes and slipped into a dreamless sleep.

Chapter 8

Facing the Neighborhood

The next morning, Tiana woke still feeling glum. At breakfast, even Charlotte's most enthusiastic attempts to cheer her up didn't help. As Big Daddy drove her home, Tiana told the LaBouffs she'd decided to cancel the party.

"Cancel?" Charlotte placed her palms on her cheeks in shock. "But you can still have a party, gumbo or no gumbo."

Tiana shook her head, miserable. "I promised everyone they would taste the *best* gumbo ever. And now I have nothing. I can't embarrass Daddy like that."

Big Daddy cleared his throat. "Tiana, there's nothing you could ever do that would embarrass your dad. He loves you more than he loves gumbo, more than he loves New Orleans, more than he loves anything. You can try your darnedest, but you can't disappoint him."

Although Tiana heard his words, they didn't land in her heart. "Thank you, Big Daddy and Charlotte, for your hospitality and your help in taking me to the market.

But it's better that you don't come tonight."

Charlotte frowned. When the car stopped in front of Tiana's house, Big Daddy got out to open her door. "You send word, and I'll have New Orleans's finest chefs over here in no time to make your dad a five-star meal. Remember: you always make your dad proud. And you make Charlotte and me proud, too."

Tiana turned her head quickly so Big Daddy wouldn't see the fresh tears springing up in her eyes. "Good-bye!" she called. The car chugged away down the street and out of sight.

Tiana wiped away her tears and trudged

into her kitchen. Her mama was at the table, sewing. She looked up in surprise. "You're home earlier than I expected. Are Charlotte and Big Daddy coming in with the gumbo?"

Tiana sat down next to her mama, studying the ribbon in her hands. Perhaps if she looked interested enough in the ribbon, her mama wouldn't notice—

"What happened? I know that face," her mama said in no time at all.

Tiana took a deep breath and told her the whole story, from the beignets, to the bargaining, to the magic sauce, to the gumbo sludge. Her mama listened, staying quiet until the story was over. "Tiana, we can go out right now and get more ingredients. I'll help you. There's still time."

Tiana shook her head. Something didn't feel right. She felt as if she'd never find the gumbo from her dream, as if everything had been turned upside down. "It's no use, Mama."

"No use? Is that what we've taught you in this house? That it's no use when something goes a little wrong to try again?" her mama asked sternly.

"No," Tiana grumbled.

"Plus, it's your daddy's birthday. He

doesn't know what you're planning, but he knows something secret is going on. We don't want to let him down, do we?"

"Mama, I feel bad enough. I know all that. . . ." Tiana turned her eyes back to the ribbon and its pretty blue sheen. Her mama didn't need magic ingredients for her dresses. Her hands and her talent made magic from ordinary things. "I know," she whispered.

Her mama picked up her sewing needle and got back to stitching. "Well, the people on this block are expecting a party. So you'll have to go and explain that there won't be any gumbo tonight."

Tiana cringed. "Do I have to?"

Tiana's mama gave her a look that said yes.

Outside, Tiana faced the first house: the new neighbor. It would be the most difficult house, the one with the person inside who didn't know her at all. Better to start with the hardest first.

Tiana gathered her strength and marched up to the front door to knock. It took a long minute, but Mrs. Marquez finally answered.

Tiana opened her mouth to explain why she was there, but the smell of smoke rising in the air made her pause. "Is something burning?"

Mrs. Marquez's eyes widened in alarm, and she raced back inside. Tiana wasn't sure whether she should follow her without invitation, but her concern won out.

Once in the kitchen, Tiana found Mrs. Marquez leaning over charred lumps on the stove. Mrs. Marquez shrugged at Tiana. "They were supposed to be beignets."

Tiana didn't know what to say. She had never seen a beignet, not even a ruined one, look like the black mess on the stove.

Mrs. Marquez shook her head. "*Ay.*

I know. I tasted one last week when I was exploring your city. So delicious, so light, it was like biting into a cloud." Mrs. Marquez threw the ruined beignets into the wastebasket. "These are more like rocks."

She sat down at the table, motioning for Tiana to join her. "I was a good baker at home. But these beignets are giving me so much trouble!" Something in Mrs. Marquez's expression matched the feeling in Tiana's heart. Not getting it right. Failing.

But then Tiana brightened. "My daddy and I make beignets all the time. I can help you!"

Mrs. Marquez smiled. "I wanted to make a perfect batch to bring to your party."

Tiana's face fell. The party. In the delight of being able to solve one problem, she'd forgotten about her own just for the moment.

"*Que pasa,* Tiana?" Mrs. Marquez asked.

"I can see on your face . . . something is not right."

Tiana felt the tears come back. Mrs. Marquez reached out and placed her hand over Tiana's. "Tell me about it."

Chapter 9
Sharing Dreams

When Tiana finished speaking, the tears weren't quite done.

"Cry all you need to. Let it out," Mrs. Marquez soothed.

Tiana wiped her eyes.

"What is your father like?" Mrs. Marquez asked.

Tiana didn't know where to start. "He loves my mama. He loves me. He loves food and cooking. We're going to have a restaurant someday. Tiana's Place."

Mrs. Marquez nodded. "He sounds like a very good father. Does he give you advice?"

Tiana grinned. "He's always giving advice. 'Work hard, Tiana.' 'Dream big, Tiana.' 'Don't take the easy way, Tiana. . . .'" Her voice trailed off. "But I did this time. Just this once, I thought maybe . . . maybe a shortcut would work. I thought it might be good to try something different. But I was wrong."

"Your father sounds very wise," Mrs. Marquez said with a smile. "And remember, never be afraid of being different or being wrong. How will you know what's right unless you make some mistakes first?" She leaned forward in her chair. "I also know something about the easy way. And some-thing about the hard way." Tiana looked up, surprised. Mrs. Marquez nodded. "In my life, the easy way was never an option. Much like what your dad says. Life is hard, dear Tiana. It will

never be easy. Not if you're doing it right. Not if you're chasing your dreams and following that evening star."

Tiana couldn't believe what she was hearing. This stranger from somewhere far away . . . she was saying the same things her daddy always said. "Is that what you did? Chase your dreams here?"

Mrs. Marquez smiled, but it was a sad smile. "Not just my dream. It was always a dream of my husband's that one day we'd end up here together. But I lost him last year. And suddenly, nothing seemed more important than getting here. Making at least part of our dream come true."

"I'm sorry about your husband," Tiana said.

"Chasing dreams can be difficult work," Mrs. Marquez continued. "Getting to this city, to this country, all the way from Cuba . . . that was nowhere near easy." She shook her head. "But it's important work." She pointed at Tiana. "And I think important work is something both you and your daddy understand well."

Tiana's heart lifted. Telling her story, having a good cry, listening to Mrs. Marquez, thinking of her daddy . . . it was making everything feel a little lighter.

"Now, enough serious talk. How about

some lunch?" Mrs. Marquez asked. "Crying can make a person very hungry. My soup is almost ready."

Tiana looked at the stove. With the smoky smell almost gone, she detected a spicy, hearty fragrance coming from a pot on the stovetop. It smelled delicious!

"Would you like to taste?" Mrs. Marquez asked, offering Tiana a spoon. "Sofrito: Spanish onions, garlic, bell peppers, tomato sauce, and a few other special spices. Just about ready to go in the broth. I make it every day. It tastes like home, and all the people I miss there."

Tiana bolted up out of her chair, eager to taste. "I know what you mean," she said, reaching for the spoon. "My daddy always says food brings people together. People from all walks of life."

Tiana took a bite of the sofrito. As the flavors hit her tongue, she was struck with an idea. There *was* a way to save her daddy's party after all!

Chapter 10
The New Plan

Tiana had a new plan. A *different* plan. But this time, it felt like the right kind of different.

"Mrs. Marquez," she said, "instead of turning this sofrito into stew, could you lend it to me?" Tiana's eye caught the sack on the counter, overflowing with white powder. "And maybe some of that flour? There's going to be a party after all."

Mrs. Marquez beamed. "But what will we eat for lunch?"

"My mama can make us sandwiches. She's really good at that!" Tiana said.

"I'll tell you what," Mrs. Marquez said. "I'll let you use my kitchen so you can keep the gumbo a secret if you show me what I'm doing wrong with these beignets."

Tiana grinned. "It's a deal!" She shook Mrs. Marquez's hand and explained her new plan. She was flooded with inspiration— maybe that evening star did have a little magic in it.

She ran across the street to her house, swinging her front door open and shouting,

"Mama!" But for the second time in a few short days, the sight of her daddy in the kitchen took her by surprise. She hadn't expected him home for hours.

"Daddy!" she exclaimed. Her father was sitting at the kitchen table, reading the newspaper and drinking coffee.

"Well, don't look so disappointed to see me, baby!" Tiana's dad held out his arms for her. Tiana ran to him. She looked over his shoulder at her mama, who was standing in the kitchen doorway.

"Happy birthday, Daddy! I didn't expect you home so soon," she said.

"I asked the boss to let me off early. On

account of wanting to spend my special day with my two favorite girls," he said.

Tiana pulled out of his hug. "Mama, can I speak to you for a moment in private?" Tiana tried to pretend this was a request she made every day as she dragged her mama into her bedroom.

"Is that secret plan bubbling back up again?" her mama asked.

"I don't have time to explain, Mama. The party is back on. You'll just have to trust me," Tiana said.

"Oh?" Her mama folded her arms and gave Tiana a look.

"Yes! Mama, I'm trying to make a dream come true. For Daddy."

Her mama considered this and finally nodded. "What do you need from me?"

"I need two sandwiches. And I need you to distract Daddy so he doesn't see me taking his gumbo pot." Tiana knew she was asking for a lot. But it had to work.

Her mama laughed. "I'll send him on an errand. And where might you be taking these sandwiches and your dad's precious pot?"

"To Mrs. Marquez's house."

Her mama raised her eyebrows.

"To make a dream come true, Mama," Tiana repeated.

"Give me two minutes." Tiana's mom winked and headed for the door.

"Make sure he's dressed up in his good suit by five p.m., too!" Tiana whispered. Then she sat on her bed and counted every second up to one hundred and twenty. Finally, she tiptoed back out into the kitchen. Her daddy was gone, and her mama was at the counter slicing bread.

It took a few moments and some wrestling, but Tiana got the gumbo pot out of the cupboard. Her mama held out two sandwiches, wrapped tight in paper. "Just put them in the pot," Tiana said. Her mama did as she asked. "Thank you!" Tiana called as she ran out the door.

Tiana needed to talk to every neighbor who was coming to the party—and fast. First stop was Grandma Marnie's. Grandma was in her usual spot in her rocking chair on the porch. "Grandma Marnie," Tiana called as she ran up the porch steps, hugging the gumbo pot. "I need a little help."

"Lucky for you, help is my specialty," Grandma Marnie said with a wink.

"I'm missing a few—well, most of my gumbo ingredients. Do you have something you can contribute? I'm making the *best* gumbo ever. Don't forget." Tiana smiled her best smile.

"A chance to contribute to the *best* gumbo ever?" Grandma Marnie said. "I'd be honored. Let me see what I've got inside."

Grandma Marnie disappeared into her house. Moments later she returned with a sack, holding it open for Tiana to see. Inside was a pile of . . . "Are those chicken bones?" Tiana asked.

"Sure are," Grandma Marnie said. "The

best soup bones you can find. I was saving them for a midweek stew, but I have a feeling they were meant to be in your gumbo."

"Thanks!" Tiana said, and she gratefully accepted the bag of bones. She moved the sandwiches and tossed the bones into the pot. Then she waved good-bye to Grandma Marnie.

Next up was the Monroe house. Tiana knocked on the door, hoping Emile wouldn't answer. But of course he did. As soon as he saw Tiana, he closed the door until she could only see a sliver of his eye.

Tiana kneeled. "Emile, I'm your friend.

Tiana, from across the way." She spoke in the sweetest voice possible. "I need a little help. Do you think you could help me?"

To her surprise, Emile nodded.

"Wonderful!" Tiana said. "Could you fetch your mama? I need some gumbo ingredients."

Emile's eye disappeared. A few moments later the door opened wider, and Annette Monroe appeared.

"Tiana," Annette said. "Will these work?" She dropped several bay leaves into the gumbo pot.

"Thank you!" Tiana said.

"Looking forward to seeing you later," Annette said.

Tiana moved down the rest of the block. Instead of telling the neighbors the party was canceled, she asked for one gumbo ingredient from each household. From the Dupres, she received a pouch of fresh sea salt. From the Potters, a handful of several divine-smelling spices. From the Keans, a large pat of freshly churned butter. From the Gilmores, the butchers, she got a handful of fresh sausage links. The Rices, to Tiana's great surprise, handed her a bag of white rice. And finally, the Wildes gave her a pail full of fresh water.

Mr. Wilde even helped her carry it back to
Mrs. Marquez's.

As she walked through Mrs. Marquez's
door, Tiana felt a surge of confidence.
Yesterday she thought she had
magic on her side, but today she
felt armed with a different kind of

magic. She had magic ingredients from the people around her. The people who always made her daddy's gumbo taste even better just by being there to share the meal.

When she reached the kitchen, Mrs. Marquez had the sofrito sizzling and ready. Tiana placed the gumbo pot on the kitchen table. As they ate their sandwiches, Tiana organized all her ingredients. Then she headed to the stove with her trusty pot and began the roux. Nothing—not the memory of yesterday's ruined gumbo or the pressure of making her daddy's night perfect—was going to let her fail now.

She added the pat of butter from the

Keans and stirred in Mrs. Marquez's flour. Slowly, surely, the roux turned the perfect shade of chocolate brown. In another pot, Tiana boiled Grandma Marnie's chicken bones in the Wildes' water with the Dupres' salt. The Gilmores' sausage went sizzling into the roux along with Mrs. Marquez's sofrito: a Cuban take on the holy vegetable trinity. Once the broth was boiling and the roux/sofrito/sausage mixture was ready, Tiana combined everything with the Monroes' bay leaves and the mysterious spices from the Potters. With the rich stew simmering, Tiana set to work helping Mrs. Marquez with the beignets.

The dough had been made just right, Tiana explained as she helped Mrs. Marquez form it into small, flat squares. The problem was that the oil was so hot, the beignets burned as soon as she dropped them in. Tiana showed Mrs. Marquez how to test the oil temperature by tearing off a tiny lump of dough and seeing how long it took to brown. They increased the fire little by little, until the lump turned gold not instantly, but within a minute. Once the oil was the right temperature, they plopped in their squares. To Mrs. Marquez's delight, the dough puffed and shimmered, turning a deep golden brown instead of charred black.

Together, they fried the beignets, coating them in powdered sugar after they came out of the oil.

Mrs. Marquez and Tiana helped themselves to one beignet each—just to make sure they were done right. Then they each had another for good measure.

After some time, Tiana tasted her own creation. The gumbo was just as good as it had been the day before, before she ruined it with the "magic" ingredient. The Rices' rice was cooked and ready for the rich brown stew to be ladled over the top. But something was still missing.

"Watch the stove, could you, Mrs.

Marquez?" Tiana asked. "I'll be right back!"

Tiana returned home. As she entered the kitchen, there her daddy was again.

"I know you're up to something, Tiana," he said behind her as she searched the cupboard. It had to be there. She couldn't not have her favorite ingredient. Not now.

There it was.

"Daddy, do you mind closing your eyes for a minute?" Tiana asked.

"Baby, as long as you aren't in any trouble, I'll close my eyes for a week." Her daddy laughed.

"I'll see you soon, Daddy!" Tiana cried, and ran back across the street. Mrs. Marquez was standing guard over the stove. Tiana looked at the bottle of hot sauce in her hands. Just enough left. She poured it into the mixture, stirred, and let it sit for a minute. She dipped the wooden spoon and tasted.

Perfect.

Chapter 11
The Feast

An hour later, Tiana was back at her house getting it ready for the party. Tiana's mama was distracting her daddy in the other room, fussing over his tie. After Tiana had swept the porch and cleared everything off the table, she swung the front door open wide, signaling to the neighborhood that the party was ready to begin.

Mrs. Marquez was the first to arrive. She balanced a tray of beignets over the top of the gumbo pot. Tiana rushed to help her, setting the gumbo down on the stove and the beignets on the table.

Then came Grandma Marnie and the rest of the Johnson family. To Tiana's surprise, Grandma Marnie was carrying several plates of her famous corn bread. "It's no party without corn bread," she said, placing the plates on the table beside the beignets.

Next the Monroes arrived. Emile approached Tiana shyly, offering her a large bowl of potato salad. "Mama says potato salad goes with everything, Miss Tiana," he said, handing her the bowl and running back to Annette.

Then came the Gilmores with a platter of hush puppies. "Every New Orleans feast has to have hush puppies," Papa Gilmore said, hugging Tiana as he put the tray on the table.

The Potters brought a large pitcher of sweet tea. The Keans contributed a mound of mashed potatoes, and the Rices brought a platter of freshly shucked corn. As dish after dish piled up next to Mrs. Marquez's beignets, it seemed the gumbo party was turning into a feast fit for a king.

Just as Tiana was about to call for her parents, Big Daddy and Charlotte walked in the door. "But I told you the party was canceled!" Tiana cried out in surprise as Charlotte covered her in hugs and blond curls. In all of the rush of re-planning the party, Tiana had completely forgotten to let them know it was back on!

"Now, Tiana," Big Daddy said with a smile. He was speaking to Tiana, but his eyes were fixed on Mrs. Marquez's platter of beignets. "We knew better than to give up on you."

Charlotte whispered, "Plus, we came by a few hours ago to check on you, and your mama told us the party was happening after all." She looked around the kitchen. "I knew you could do it, Tiana. I'm sorry I distracted you with that silly magic stuff."

"I had a hand in that, too, Lottie. No one made me buy that sauce but me," Tiana said.

"It turned out for the best, though."

Charlotte pulled a sack from her arm. "We brought something, too." She opened the bag to reveal a mound of crab. She plucked one out and held it in the air.

"You didn't have to do that," Tiana said as she clasped the sack. "Thank you, Big Daddy."

Big Daddy grinned, his mouth covered in sugar.

Tiana emptied the bag into the still-simmering gumbo. "I think it's time," she whispered to the crowd gathered in her kitchen and spilling out onto the porch.

She crept down the hallway to her parents' bedroom.

"Daddy? Could you come out to the kitchen for a moment?" Tiana asked.

"You finally want to show me what you've been up to?" Her daddy reached a hand out to Tiana, and she took it in her own and led him to the kitchen.

"Surprise!" everyone shouted.

Her daddy laughed and laughed and laughed. Tiana wasn't sure whether he was surprised, but she *was* sure he was happy. "You did all this for me?" he asked.

"I wanted to make you the best party

ever. The best gumbo ever," Tiana said.

Her dad looked at the table. "Something's for sure—this is going to be the best meal I've ever eaten. I can tell just by looking." He squeezed Tiana's hand. "Where's this gumbo I'm smelling?"

This was it—the moment Tiana had seen in her dream. She was surrounded by all the neighborhood families—Big Daddy, Charlotte, her new friend Mrs. Marquez, her mama, and especially her daddy. It was better than her dream. It was real.

"Have a taste, Daddy," Tiana said, handing him a spoon.

"Did you make this all by yourself?" he asked.

"I made it—but I had help," Tiana said. "From everyone here. Even you."

Her daddy dipped the spoon into the gumbo pot and lifted it to his mouth. He tasted, swallowed, and smacked his lips.

"Mmmm-mm, Tiana," he said. "That is, without a doubt, the *best* gumbo ever."

Tiana wrapped her arms around her daddy in a giant hug. He'd said the words she'd been longing to hear. As she held him tight, something about the gumbo caught her eye.

She was sure it had sparkled.

Disney
Before the Story

Cinderella
TAKES THE STAGE

By
TESSA ROEHL

Illustrated By
ADRIENNE BROWN

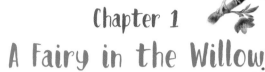

Chapter 1
A Fairy in the Willow

Ella stared into the willow tree, looking for a twinkle, a glow, or the movement of wings. "Are you sure there are fairies in this tree, Mother?" Ella asked.

"Yes, quite sure," her mother replied.

Ella frowned. The only wings she could see belonged to the songbirds. Ella came to this bench every day to watch the animals. She was sure if there were fairies around, she would have noticed. But just in case, she looked harder.

This was Ella's favorite corner of the garden because there was a feeling here that anything was possible. In this corner, a pear tree had borne fruit after a winter's frost, a rabbit had nibbled a berry right from her hand, and two hazel branches had grown twisting around each other, as if they couldn't stand to be apart.

That Ella could also see the highest tower of the King's castle from her garden bench didn't hurt either. With a view of a place where royalty lived, ruling so lovingly over Ella's tiny kingdom, it was easy to get swept

away in daydreams. The songbirds knew all about Ella's dreams, because sometimes she simply had to tell someone.

She would tell the birds about the castle's magnificent sparkling staircase. She'd heard that it was just inside the Grand Hall.

Someday, she said, she would float down the steps while someone very important announced her name.

She would tell the birds about the dress, too. It would be made of silver and gold fabric, just like the one in the window of the village dressmaker's shop. The one she would buy with the money she planned to win at the Midsummer Festival Puppet Contest.

The birds would only chirp in reply. And they never told Ella any of their dreams. So she often wished for a different kind of friend to share her dreams with.

On days like this, when Ella found

herself wishing for things that were not there, she was glad to have the company of her mother—even if she was just talking about fairies she couldn't see.

One thing Ella could see was an army of ants marching across the garden, right in the path of her shoe. The thought of all those tiny feet crawling up her stocking made Ella squirm.

Ella gathered her legs to her chest as the ants scurried into their anthill. But before she could return her shoes to the ground, she noticed that one ant was left behind, running in circles around the base of the bench.

"Ella, dear," her mother said. "Has this little ant frightened you?"

"I don't want it to crawl on me," Ella said, still hugging her knees.

Ella's mother pointed to the ant. "Who might be the more terrified one in this garden? The one who has lost sight of his family and forgotten his way? Or you, with your size and your mother to protect you?"

She opened her fan, which she always carried on warm days like this one. Blue and red painted petunias blossomed against thin cream paper.

She laid the fan against the ground. The ant crawled into a fold, and Ella's mother carried it to the anthill.

The ant disappeared into the dirt.

"Everyone deserves a happy ending," her mother said as she sat back down.

"I don't mind the ants. I just don't want to touch them," Ella said.

Ella's mother pulled her close. "Ella, when you were new to the world, I would bring you out to this bench and sing to you every morning."

"I like it when you sing." Ella rested her head on her mother's shoulder. She hoped the ant had found its way back to its own mother.

"I sang so that the fairies would listen. I sang songs about my dreams for you, hoping there might be a fairy who would take a special interest in my little Ella. And then, one day, a fairy did."

"In me?" Ella's eyes opened wide.

"She flew out of the willow tree, dressed in a blue frock. She asked if she could be your fairy godmother," Ella's mother said.

Ella had never heard of such a thing. "And what did you say?"

"Silly dear. I said yes!" Ella's mother laughed. "And she said, 'Tell Ella, this is her fairy godmother's tree. Should she ever need some magic, she'll know where to find it.'"

"Is this a real story?" Ella looked up at her mother's smiling face.

"Do you want it to be real, my darling?" her mother asked.

"Of course I do!" Ella exclaimed.

"So then it's real. Anything can be real if you believe it." Ella's mother winked.

Ella considered this. "But, Mother. Why did you want the fairies to take an interest in me?"

"I will always be looking out for you,

my Ella," her mother said. "But I knew it wouldn't hurt if someone with a touch of magic was looking out for you as well. We must always look out for others. Especially the smallest creatures."

"Arf!" A bark followed by a series of loud, splashing crashes sounded across the garden.

"And speaking of small creatures." Ella's mother stood. "I think your new puppy could use some looking after."

Ella sighed as her mother left the garden. Bruno had knocked over several watering cans, creating a perfect, puppy-sized mud pit. And Bruno liked mud.

"Oh, Bruno." Ella picked him up, careful

to avoid his dirty fur.
She couldn't help
smiling as she carried
him to the barn. He whined but stayed still
as she washed him.

"Now, let's hurry up and have lunch," Ella
told him. "No more playing about with fairies
for me, and no more playing about with mud
for you. I have to finish my puppets in time
to win the contest." Bruno barked in response
and then bounded up the path behind her,
toward the chateau.

Chapter 2
An Unwanted Visitor

Ella entered the dining room just as her parents were sitting down at the table. She eyed the platter in the middle: roasted fish and vegetables—it wasn't her favorite meal, but it was certainly one of Bruno's.

Ella kissed her father on the cheek as she headed toward the kitchen to retrieve Bruno's lunch. She hadn't taken two steps before Florence, the cook, appeared with Bruno's bowl in her hands.

"Thank you, Florence. Bruno thanks you, too!" Ella took the bowl and placed it under the table. Florence smiled at Ella and retreated to the kitchen. Ella looked at the colorless mush that made up Bruno's lunch. She'd make sure to sneak him some of the fish.

Ella took her place at the table next to her mother.

She loaded her plate with a small portion and chewed fast enough that she wouldn't taste it. In no time, her plate was empty.

"All that chatting in the garden with your mother worked up an appetite, did it, Ella?" Her father looked at her, amused. He wasn't even halfway done with his serving.

"There's really no time to waste, Father. If I'm going to win the puppet contest, every minute counts," Ella said. She scooped a bit more of the fish onto her plate. As her father leaned in for another bite, Ella sneaked a piece down to Bruno's waiting mouth.

"It's hard to believe you're already old enough to enter," Ella's mother said.

"I've only been waiting for this my entire life!" Ella said. "It's my favorite time of year."

Ella's mother chuckled. "We know it's your favorite, darling. When you were younger, I had a terrible time pulling you away from the festival bonfires. You were so enchanted that you would come home covered in cinders."

"Cinders?" Ella asked. "I love the bonfires, but I don't remember getting dirty."

"I remember," Ella's father chimed in.

"Your father had to rinse you off, just like you were a puppy splashing in the mud." Ella's mother tousled Ella's hair. "Our little Cinderella."

Ella scowled playfully. Bruno licked her hand below the table, tasting fish. Ella was hoping she would be excused—soon.

"How are your puppets coming along?" Ella's father asked.

"They're all right. I'm having a touch of trouble making them look the way they do in my head." Ella was stretching the truth. She was actually having nothing but trouble.

"I do wish I could help you," her mother said. "I never took to sewing myself. It just wasn't my cup of tea, I suppose."

"I'll sort it out. How hard can it be to make little costumes and little puppets?"

Ella asked. She slipped one more bite of fish to Bruno and then fidgeted in her chair.

"You're excused, Ella. Run along to work your magic," Ella's father said, as if reading her mind. "I brought a couple of things for you from the village, by the way. They're on the desk in my study."

Ella leaped up from her chair. "Oh, thank you, Father!" She hurried to the desk. Folded on top were a piece of plum-colored velvet and a length of black ribbon. They would be perfect for the frog puppet's suit.

With her new materials in hand, Ella left the house and ran toward the barn. Bruno trailed behind.

"Good luck, my Cinderella!" Ella heard her mother call from an open window. Ella turned back and waved.

The chickens clucked around Ella's ankles as she passed.

"I know you've all had your lunch already." Ella winked at the birds and dipped her hand into a pail of corn. She tossed a handful onto the ground. Bruno tried to pick up some kernels, but the chickens kept beating him to it. Ella wagged her finger at him. "If you get extra lunch today, I think they should, too."

Inside the barn, Ella made her way to the corner where she'd set up her workplace. She added the new fabric and ribbon to the pile of other materials:

ribbons and beads,

pieces of linen,

MORE trimmings,

and a handful of buttons.

It was everything Ella needed to make beautiful puppets.

If only she could actually make them.

Ella tried not to look at the other pile on the table. It was a collection of misshapen puppet heads and tiny costumes filled with holes from her frustrated stitches. She sat down on her stool, set her shoulders back, and held her head high. No matter about the pile of mistakes. Ella was certain she could figure out how to fix them.

She picked up the puppet that was supposed to be the maiden. It looked more like a potato.

She had just set to ripping out the stitches when she heard a clatter outside the barn. Ella dropped the puppet. She turned around to scold Bruno for whatever he had gotten into this time, but Bruno was right there on the ground, snoozing.

Ella ran to the barn door and saw what had caused the commotion. Next to the doorway was a metal bucket of discarded sewing scraps. The bucket was lying on its side—and it was empty. Ella looked around to see what animal might have knocked it over. But instead she saw a girl running away toward the trees beyond the chateau gate.

Thief! Ella thought. And before she had time to think anything else, Ella sprinted after her.

Chapter 3
A Failed Escape

"**H**ey! Come back!" Ella shouted as she ran. The excitement had awakened Bruno, and he raced alongside her. The girl disappeared into the trees just as Ella reached the edge of the woods. Ella wasn't used to chasing people, or going into the woods, for that matter. She was about to turn back when she saw the girl again. The thief had stopped running. She was standing, hands on hips, only a few trees away.

Ella marched toward the thief. As she got closer, she could see that the girl's clothes were tattered, her face was grubby, and her short, dark hair was chopped unevenly. She didn't seem to notice as Ella approached.

The girl was just looking at the ground and . . . talking to it?

"Excuse me! What do you think you're—Oh!" Ella had reached the thief, who wasn't talking to the ground at all. She was talking to a small, brown-spotted pig whose foot was caught on a tree root. Bruno sniffed the pig.

"Now look what you've done, Claudio," the thief said to the pig. The pig squealed in response.

"Surely it's not his fault," Ella said, forgetting for a moment why she had chased the girl into the forest. "Here, if both of us pull on the root, I think we can give him enough space to wiggle out."

The two girls grabbed hold of the root and tugged as hard as they could. It was thick and tough, but it rose enough to give Claudio room to move. He didn't budge, however. He stayed there, staring at Ella.

"Claudio, enough! Move!" the thief urged her pig. Bruno let out one of his best barks.

Claudio squealed and jumped away from the root.

"That's a good boy," Ella said to the pig, holding her hand out to say hello.

Claudio nuzzled her palm and let out a soft snort.

"This is all his fault." The thief gave Claudio a scratch under his chin. "He does this kind of thing on purpose. Doesn't think it's right to run away and all that. This pig's morals are too strong for his own good," the thief said as she picked Claudio up and plopped him in her bag.

Ella suddenly remembered she was angry. "Well, at least one of you has some morals. What gives you the right to steal from me?"

The thief rolled her eyes. "Steal? That wasn't stealing. You weren't using those scraps. You were throwing them away!"

"That doesn't make them yours!" Ella said.

"It doesn't matter anyway. You can have them back." The thief dug into the satchel slung over her shoulder. It was actually a flour sack attached to an old leather belt. "I didn't even realize what I was taking. I could have saved us both some trouble, because these are definitely not my taste—Cinderella."

She shoved a handful of the discarded beads and fabric toward Ella, who accepted them with a huff.

The thief stomped off in the direction of the village. Bruno barked after them. "Hush, Bruno. They're not your friends," Ella scolded him. From inside the thief's bag, Claudio snorted at Ella and Bruno. He really was quite cute. Ella shook her head. Never mind. She stomped back home.

Chapter 4
A Search in the Village

lla arrived back at the chateau to find
her parents having tea in the sitting room.
She was out of breath from her chase into
the woods and her angry return. She flung
herself onto the sofa.

"Well, that was a short work session,"
Ella's father said as he stirred a spoonful of
sugar into his teacup.

"I didn't do any work," Ella grumbled.

Ella's mother crossed the room and put her hand to Ella's cheek. "Darling, are you all right? Your face is flushed."

Ella patted her mother's hand. "That's because I've been chasing down a thief when I ought to have been perfecting my puppets."

Seeing her parents' confused faces, Ella told them the story of her encounter with the girl in the woods: from the clattering bucket, to the stuck pig, to her retreat. "I'm too distracted now to get any work done today," she finished. "And it's all her fault."

Ella's parents shared a look. The kind of look they didn't think Ella noticed, but she always did. It meant they knew something Ella didn't.

"What?" Ella asked. "Why aren't you as angry as I am? Don't you think stealing is wrong?"

Ella's father cleared his throat and set down his tea. "Ella, my sunshine, it's true that these were materials you discarded."

"But that doesn't give her the right—" Ella began.

Her father held up a hand, silencing her. "Ella, you'll often find that people deserve more than one encounter before you rush to judgment. This girl, whom you call a thief, why, she's more than just a thief. She's a pig owner. She's a forest traveler. You can't know that she meant you harm when she took your scraps." Ella's father handed her a cup of tea. "There's good in everyone. You just have to know where to find it," he added.

Ella tasted her tea. Her father always made it just right, with the perfect amount of milk and sugar.

"What do you think, dear? Do you hear what your father is saying?" Ella's mother asked.

"Yes, Mother. Yes, Father. I hear you." Ella continued sipping her tea. *Good in everyone?* she thought. The look on the thief's face when she sneered at Ella's scraps—that wasn't very good.

Yes, Ella heard her parents. But she didn't have to agree.

The next morning when Ella woke, her father's words were still on her mind. They had been there all night, worming their way into her dreams. She also couldn't stop picturing the face of the little pig, Claudio. He really was cute. And so small. Considering the thief's shabby appearance,

Ella worried whether the pig had enough to eat.

She decided that instead of her morning daydream in the garden, she'd go to the village to find poor, possibly hungry Claudio. Ella slurped down her breakfast, rushed to help her mother with the chores, and gathered a small bag of grain. She had just set off down the path to the village when Bruno trotted up beside her.

"Bruno," Ella said as she stopped. "Wouldn't you rather stay home and play in the garden? I won't be gone long."

Bruno licked Ella's hands and wagged his tail.

Ella thought for a moment. "You've never been to the village before. You'll have to stay out of trouble. But maybe you can help sniff out that pig and make sure he knows we're his friends. Do you think you can do that?"

Bruno yelped and wagged his tail harder.

"All right, then. Come along, and keep your eyes and nose out for Claudio."

Ella and Bruno continued down the path. Bruno paused every few steps to enjoy a new scent. "I think you'll like the village," Ella said as they walked. "There are many things to smell, people to meet, and crumbs to eat. Just don't get any ideas about making a mess."

They reached the first line of shops, and Ella tried not to feel nervous. She rarely went to the village alone, and she wasn't sure where to begin. All she had was a description of a girl and a pig.

Gathering her courage, she approached the first person she saw: a man selling fresh bread from his cart.

"Excuse me, have you seen a girl with short, dark hair? Kind of dirty, wears a flour sack, and carries a pet pig?" As she spoke, Ella realized there couldn't possibly be more than one person who fit that description.

"Hmmm." The man thought. "Girl, yes. Pig, no. Try the west side of the village. I believe she comes from that direction."

Ella gave a little curtsy. "Thank you."

She and Bruno headed west. As they went, she asked a few more people. Again, no one had seen Claudio, but they seemed familiar with the girl. One shopkeeper pointed Ella toward a large estate looming atop a small hill.

Ella was sure he was mistaken. She couldn't imagine the thief living in such a grand home. But with nothing else to go on, Ella and Bruno headed up the drive. As they approached the gate, Ella began quietly calling out, "Claudio! Claudio!"

They were almost to the top of the hill. Bruno's ears pricked up and his nose twitched. It seemed they were getting closer. "Claudio!" Ella cried a bit louder.

Suddenly, the thief appeared in front of her. And before Ella knew it, she was being yanked off the drive.

Chapter 5
Metal, Moss, and Stone

Ella had been pulled into a small room. Or not just a room. A one-room home. A shack, really. The thief stood in front of Ella, her face angry. Bruno nosed open the door and sauntered inside, heading for a bed against the wall.

"What do you think you're doing?" Ella asked the thief.

"What am *I* doing? What do you think

you're doing?" the thief responded, hands on hips.

"I was looking for Claudio," Ella said. As she spoke his name, the little pig crawled out from under the bed. There was only one in the room, as well as a small stove, a modest table with two chairs, and curtains draped across a corner.

That was it. *Does someone really live here?* Ella wondered.

"Listen, you can't go around shouting his name." The thief picked up the pig, and he snuffled her cheek. She placed a hand over Claudio's head, covering his ears. "My mother and I live here. We take care of all the animals on the property: pigs, sheep, cows, chickens. The master of the estate can't know about Claudio."

"Why not? Did you steal him, too?" Ella asked, putting her hands on her hips.

"Stealing isn't always bad, you know." The thief pressed her hands harder against the pig's ears. "Claudio was born to a pair of the estate owner's prized pigs. He was the tiniest runt any of us had ever seen. The instant Sir Edgard saw him, he ordered my mother to"—the girl shuddered—"dispose of him. Of course we couldn't do that. So I took him. Sir Edgard can't find out, or I don't know what he'll do."

Ella could not believe what she was hearing. Not just the story about Claudio, but the name: Sir Edgard. Ella was sure she'd heard it before. Then it dawned on her. "Why, Sir Edgard! The judge of the puppet contest? That Sir Edgard?"

The girl narrowed her eyes at Ella. "The very one. I'm not even so sure he's a sir.

He certainly tells us to call him that, but I can't imagine the good king making that awful man a sir."

"Oh, my." Ella couldn't stand to think that the man who had been cruel to Claudio would be the same person to judge her puppets. But what could she do about it? She handed the bag of grain to the girl. "Anyway. This is why I came. I wanted to make sure Claudio had enough to eat."

The girl looked at the gift. Claudio struggled in her arms to peek into the bag. "He does just fine. Claudio eats even before my mother and I do. But thank you anyway."

Ella shrugged and headed for the door. The girl called after her. "Wait. I'm sorry. I didn't introduce myself. My name is Val, short for Valentine."

Ella turned. "You know, my name isn't actually Cinderella. That was just a silly name you must have heard my mother call me. My real name is Ella."

Val waved her hand as if to dismiss what Ella said. "You really ought to stick with Cinderella, for the contest. You're entering, right? I never go by Valentine, but that's what I'm using for the contest. It's a much better puppeteer name, and so is Cinderella. Mademoiselle Cinderella."

Ella was surprised. "You're entering the contest?"

Val set Claudio on the floor, along with the bag of grain. Bruno had been waiting at her feet for the pig and sniffed him hello. "Can I show you something?"

"Of course." Ella was curious.

Val walked to the curtains hanging in the corner and pulled them to the side. A stack of crates was shoved against the wall, piled high with various puppets. Puppets like Ella had never seen before. Made from materials she had never seen before. Where Ella had been using fabric, thread, stuffing,

and lace, Val's puppets were made from all kinds of materials.

"Your puppets—they're glorious," Ella could only whisper.

"They're getting there," Val said. "Thank you, though. Once I win the contest, I plan to buy a goat with the gold coin."

"A goat?" Ella crinkled her nose. She thought it seemed like a strange prize.

Val nodded, excited. "My mother has been saving to buy a farm out in the country. So we can get away from Sir Edgard once and for all. Of course, that's a long way off, considering how little he pays her. He's always finding reasons to dock her wages, too. A goat would be a good start. One animal of our own. Besides Claudio."

Ella had never thought about what it might be like to want to escape your home and start again somewhere new. But it made sense for Val. "Well, if you can finish them, you might have a good chance at winning."

Val sighed. "Yes. I wish I had more room to work. But I'll get them done. I believe it."

Ella wanted to touch the puppets and examine them. She wanted to see how Val managed to sew leaves together when Ella couldn't even attach a button. Then an idea formed in Ella's mind. "Val, I have a proposal for you."

"You have a proposal for a thief?" Val smirked.

"I think there's a way we can help each other," Ella said.

"I'm listening, Cinderella."

Ella smiled. "I'm having a little . . . trouble working with my materials. Sewing anything, really. If you show me some of your tricks, I'd like to offer you space in my barn to work on your puppets. There's plenty of room for both of us! And I promise I won't copy your ideas, as long as you don't copy mine."

Val chuckled. "I've got plenty of ideas. I won't be taking yours." She scratched her head, thinking. "It's a deal!" she said, sticking out her hand.

Ella shook Val's hand, pleased with her own clever thinking. "Excellent. I'll see you tomorrow morning, first thing."

"Claudio and I will be there!" Val said. Claudio didn't look up from the food he was devouring.

Ella and Bruno left the shack. Val's puppets were going to be hard to beat. But Ella still believed her own puppets could win. Now that she would have help, she was sure she was closer than ever to winning the gold coin. As they walked back through the village toward the chateau, she waved at the dress in the window that would soon be hers.

Chapter 6
An Unusual Set of Tools

The next morning, just after breakfast, Val arrived at the chateau, pulling a makeshift wagon. It was filled to the brim with puppet parts and other odds and ends. Ella couldn't wait to see how Val would use the strange assortment of things.

"Where do you want us?" Val asked, lifting Claudio out of the flour satchel on her shoulder. The pig ran into the barn as if he'd lived there for years. Bruno followed him, sniffing eagerly all the way.

"Here." Ella took the wagon handle from Val and walked inside, where she'd set up a table identical to her own.

"Wow. There sure is a lot of space." Val unloaded her cart, piling up pieces of wood, broken door handles, chain links, part of a horse blanket, flower petals, and more. Ella tried not to stare, but she was curious.

"Oh!" Val jumped back, dropping the broken leather shoe she was unpacking. "Hello?"

A furry brown head had popped up in the pile of Val's supplies.

"That's just one of the barn mice," Ella said. "They're quite friendly!"

The mouse scurried into the pile. "No problem, mouse," Val said. "You may want to avoid this table. It could be dangerous if you dart over here while I'm hammering."

"Hammering?" Ella shook her head in amazement. She sat down at her own table and picked up the maiden puppet, which still looked like a potato. She squished the stuffed shape near the bottom. She hoped if she attacked it with a needle and thread, she might be able to form a neck. A neck that would lead to a head.

After she'd jabbed the puppet a few

times, she noticed that the clanking and scraping of Val's unloading had stopped. Ella turned and startled. Val was right behind her, watching her hands.

"I see your problem, Cinderella," Val said, a smile forming on her face.

"Am I completely hopeless?" Ella asked.

Val shook her head and sat down. "You just need some basics."

Val showed Ella how to begin a stitch and how to knot it at the end. In no time, Val had a neat, strong seam forming a neck that looked like a neck. Then a head that looked like a head. Ella paid close attention.

"How would you sew something like

this?" Ella held up a piece of her favorite fabric, a shiny blue silk. Part of it was covered in holes where Ella had accidentally torn the fabric with her needle.

"Well, that's very delicate." Val retrieved some things from her supplies and brought them to Ella. "Take this rose petal, for example. Not an easy thing to sew with that large metal needle. But this can keep it from tearing." Val pulled a thin threaded pine needle through the rose petal, creating a few perfect stitches down the middle. "Try it!"

"A pine needle!" Ella was shocked. Val was full of surprises.

"Of course!" Val said. "You'd be surprised

what makes itself available to you when you're in need. I use all the tools at my disposal. Even if they don't seem like tools at first." Val smiled. She gave Ella a handful of pine needles and sat back down to her own puppets.

"Now, where is the thread I wanted to use for this silk? It's a lovely blue. It looks like a wisp of sky." Ella searched through her things. Another barn mouse crept out from under some fabric. The spool of sky-blue thread was balanced on his head. "Why, thank you," Ella told the mouse as she took the spool.

Ella picked up one of the pine needles. She wasn't sure how Val had made such a perfect hole for the thread. The mouse sat, watching Ella think. His eyes were bright and curious. "Any ideas?" Ella asked the mouse as she held the needle out for him to see. The mouse bit into the end of the pine needle and scurried away before Ella could react.

She looked at the needle. The mouse's tooth had made a tiny hole in the end—just the right size. Ella threaded the pine needle and poked it through the silk. She found that even when she tugged, the fabric stayed in one piece. "It's working. You're a genius, Val!"

"I can't disagree with you," Val said.

"Where did you learn all this?" Ella

asked as she continued weaving the pine needle through the fabric. She was making what she hoped would be the maiden's skirt.

"My mother taught me ages ago. If she didn't, I wouldn't have any clothes to wear!" Val spoke between loud bangs as she beat a brick with a hammer.

Ella couldn't imagine what she was going to do with pieces of brick.

"Sorry," Val said. "Is this noise going to bother you?"

Ella shook her head. "If you want, I really do have plenty of materials here. You're welcome to use some of them."

"No, thanks." Val returned to her brick.

"They're very pretty. But I think I have a style of my own going here. Now that I have room to actually swing my hammer."

Ella finished the hem of the skirt. The next step in her plan was a lace top. She began looking for a piece of lace, but stopped. *Use all the tools at your disposal.* "Excuse me, little mouse? Are you there?"

The mouse curiously crawled out of the fabric pile.

"Do you happen to know where the ivory lace is? I think I brought it in a couple of days ago," Ella told the mouse, who darted back into the pile. He returned moments later, the lace in his teeth. Ella was delighted. "Why, thank you! Do you have a name?"

The mouse stared at her, whiskers twitching.

"I see. Well, let's call you Leopold. Leo for short," Ella said as she patted his head.

The mouse bowed and ran back to the mound of materials, squeaking. Ella could have sworn that the squeak sounded just like the mouse had said, "Good day, Cinderella."

Ella turned to Val.
"Did you hear that?
I'm sure that mouse
spoke to me. Have you ever heard a mouse
speak?"

"Hmm, I don't think so." Val shrugged.
"Maybe a fairy charmed him."

The girls continued working for hours,
pausing only for the soup Florence brought
them for lunch. Val sewed and hammered
and fastened. Ella sewed and cut and beaded.

By the time the sun was low in the sky,
Ella's maiden puppet was nearly finished.
The girls took a break for tea and biscuits
brought out by Ella's father. He didn't say a

word to interrupt. He just gave the two girls, Claudio, and Bruno pats on the head and a tip of his hat.

"So, what would you do with the prize money, Mademoiselle Cinderella?" Val asked as she sipped her tea.

"What *will* I do with the prize money, you mean?" Ella grinned.

"I admit you've made a lot of progress. But I have a trick up my sleeve that will guarantee me the win," Val said.

"Oh, do you?" Ella took a sip of tea. "It's not just about the gold coin for me. The Midsummer Festival is my favorite day of the year. There's so much magic in the air. And the puppets are the best part—besides the bonfires, of course." She paused. For some reason, she felt silly telling Val about the dress. "But the prize is a bonus. I've had my eye on a dress in the village. I guess that might seem less important than a goat."

Val's eyes lit up. "Is it the gold-and-silver one? In the window of Madame Colette's?"

"Yes!" Ella was surprised. Val didn't seem like the type to care about a dress. She could make such beautiful things herself.

"It's absolutely gorgeous. It would look stunning with your hair," Val said.

Ella blushed.

Val continued. "I don't think a dream of winning a dress is any less important than a dream of winning a goat. We should all get the chance, right? Our hearts don't always need to want the same thing. As long as they want something."

Ella felt much better. Val understood. "Exactly," Ella said.

"I'm just sorry your dream won't come true this year," Val said with a smirk Ella now knew well.

"Oh, you." Ella threw a handful of hay at Val.

"Thank you! This will make fabulous puppet hair," Val said, giggling.

The girls finished their tea. Claudio and Bruno were fast asleep on the hay after a day of playing. Val scooped the sleeping Claudio into her bag, and held out her hand for Ella to shake. "Same time tomorrow?" Val asked.

"Same time," Ella said. She waved good-bye as Val and Claudio trotted down the path toward the village. Ella felt warm inside, and it wasn't only from the tea.

Chapter 7
A Partner in Puppets and Dreams

The next day, Val showed up again, as promised. And the day after that, and the day after that—and every day leading up to the festival.

Val and Ella worked side by side. They talked about everything. Val told Ella about living with her mother on Sir Edgard's estate. Val's mother used to care for the animals with Val's father, and each earned a salary. After Val's father died, Val's mother had to take on double the work—but Sir Edgard refused to give her double the pay. Val tried to help her mother whenever she could, but Sir Edgard felt he was so important that he wouldn't speak to Val directly. He would pass orders to her through her mother, saying things like "Tell the child this" or "Tell the child that."

Val told Ella about what her future farm would look like: not too big and not too small. There would be some geese, a cow, some chickens, and Val's goat, to start. Val talked about how peaceful the farm would be. She and her mother would feel so free. There would be no one like Sir Edgard to give them orders. The work they did would be only for themselves.

In turn, Ella shared her dreams with Val. She told Val of her morning visits to the garden, looking for the fairies and gazing at the castle. How she pictured herself dancing in the castle ballroom or even atop one of the clouds in the sky. Ella also dreamed of experiencing a great adventure someday. The kind of adventure that might be written down in books like the ones she read with her father in his study. She told Val how she couldn't wait to grow up and see more of the world beyond their lovely but small kingdom.

It occurred to Ella that only days before, she had been sitting in the garden, longing for someone to talk to and share her dreams with. And maybe she had stumbled upon a pocket of magic, because that very person had entered her life. As Val had said, *You'd be surprised what makes itself available to you when you're in need.* Ella hadn't even realized how much she needed Val, but here Val was all the same.

Bruno and Claudio also had become fast friends. They would dart around the beams and buckets and piles of hay, playing hide-and-seek and sharing bits of food. Then they would curl up together to nap in the warm afternoon sun that shone through the barn window.

That was how it went day after day. As Claudio and Bruno played and napped, Ella and Val chatted and worked. All the while, Val would offer Ella tips on how to craft her puppets. Leo and the rest of the barn mice proved helpful as well. They would line up with the exact materials Ella needed before she even knew to look for them. Soon Ella had nearly all her puppets complete.

There were a frog, a maiden,

a fairy, and a tree.

Ella couldn't figure out what Val's puppets were supposed to be, and Val wouldn't tell her. All Ella knew was that it didn't matter. They were magnificent. Ella kept offering Val some of her beads or trimmings or fabric. Val kept refusing, always saying something like "I've got everything I need. Don't worry about me, Cinderella."

At the end of their last working day, on the eve of the festival, Ella sat back in her chair, admiring her puppets. She was tired but still had the tingle of excitement she always felt the night before a holiday.

Val packed her own finished puppets into her wagon. For the first time, the girls hugged goodbye instead of shaking hands.

Val tucked Claudio into the flour satchel

and called out as she walked down the path, "Tomorrow is the big day! The village won't know what's coming to them. Cinderella and Valentine, master puppeteers!"

As Ella watched Val leave, her heart felt heavy. She was full of love for her new friend and for Claudio. Ella yearned to see Val's dreams come true as much as her own. But she was also confused. She didn't feel any different about her own goal. She still wanted that win and the dress that came with it.

Ella wondered, how could both of their dreams come true when they were competing against each other for one prize?

Chapter 8
An Appeal for Magic

Later that evening, after supper, Ella left a sleeping Bruno by the fireplace and made her way to the garden bench. She hadn't visited her corner of the garden since Val's visits had begun.

Ella's thoughts swirled around in her mind. Her dreams had always felt so clear and so much her own. But now they were mixed up with someone else's.

Ella sat down on the bench and faced the willow. This time she didn't stare and wait for the fairies to appear. She spoke to them. "Fairy Godmother, I know you're in there. My mother told me about you. That you're looking out for me. But I've found someone else who needs looking after. Her name is Val, and she has a pig named Claudio. I'm sure you'd like them. I didn't like her so much at first, but . . . never mind."

Ella thought about what she was asking for. "I thought since you have magic on your side, maybe you could help us. We both want to win the puppet contest tomorrow. I don't know how it's possible for both of us to get what we want. And even if Val wins, I fear it's not enough to reach her dream of a farm in the country. Can you help her get that farm, Fairy Godmother? At the very least, could you make sure we stay friends no matter who wins? Or help Sir Edgard to stop being so cruel?"

Ella had closed her eyes. She opened one, just a little, hoping she might see a fairy in a blue frock before her. Nothing. She opened both eyes. Still nothing.

Ella's shoulders fell. She didn't understand. Had her mother made it all up?

She felt a hand touch her shoulder. Without looking, she knew who it was.

"Ella, darling. She is there. She's always there."

"It doesn't look at all like she's there, Mother," Ella said.

Her mother sat down and took her hands. "Your fairy godmother will always be here for you. I promise you that much. You must

have faith. She will appear to you when you need her the most."

"When will that be?" Ella asked.

Her mother tucked a lock of hair behind Ella's ear. "I hope not anytime soon. But it's very kind of you to ask for help for Val."

"I didn't think it could hurt to try," Ella said.

"Of course not," Ella's mother said. "Though it may make you happy to know that Val's dreams have a magic and power of their own, as all dreams do. Why, I wouldn't be surprised if she has her own fairy godmother."

"Oh, that would be wonderful," Ella said.

"You don't always have to look to the willow tree." Ella's mother put her hand over Ella's heart. "Friendship and love have their own magical way of helping wishes come true."

Ella hoped her mother was right. A farm was such a big dream for someone who had to hide a tiny pig. And it seemed that one way or another, Val or Ella would end up disappointed by the end of the festival. But then Ella caught sight of the glowing castle towers in the distance and felt her heart leap. *Anything is possible,* she reminded herself.

And the possibilities would start tomorrow, when Mademoiselle Cinderella and Mademoiselle Valentine premiered their puppet shows at the Midsummer Festival.

Chapter 9
A Festival of Surprises

The next morning, Ella woke before the sun rose. The day of the festival had arrived. She felt as though one of her beloved bonfires were sparking up inside her chest. She rushed through her morning routine so she could begin loading her puppets into her father's wagon. Ella felt so impatient that she thought about trying to drive the horses herself while her father searched for his hat. But she didn't want to risk crashing the wagon and harming the puppets.

After what felt like forever, Ella, her mother, her father, Bruno, and the puppets headed toward the village. Ella's excitement swelled as they drew closer. She could hear the music, smell the treats, and see the colorful festival banners draped across the rooftops. As soon as her father pulled the wagon to a stop, Ella jumped down and ran to find the puppet booths.

She found Val with her mother, already setting up. "Cinderella, here!" Val pointed at the booth next to hers. "I made sure it stayed empty. Oh, and this is my mother."

Val's mother waved at Ella. She had the same dark hair as Val, and the same kind eyes and playful smile.

Ella returned her wave. "It's a pleasure to meet you, Madame. I've heard so much about you."

"As have I, love," Val's mother said. "I'm looking forward to seeing the shows you girls have cooked up in that barn. Val won't tell me a thing!"

Val's mother helped Val lift one of her puppets behind the booth. Ella noticed that it had a stick fastened to the bottom. Ella had wondered how Val was planning to operate it. Ella's puppets had places to hide a hand inside or strings attached. Val must have attached the stick when she left the barn, no doubt part of her much-talked-about "secret."

Ella's mother and father approached, her father carrying her crate of puppets. Ella got busy setting up in the booth next to Val's as her parents introduced themselves to Val's mother.

"Okay, everyone. Time to enjoy the festival and leave Mademoiselle Valentine and Mademoiselle Cinderella to their debuts. So long!" Val signaled for their parents to leave.

Ella's mother laughed and kissed Ella on the forehead. "Shine like the fairies are watching, my darling," she said.

"I'm proud of you, Ella," her father said. "Excuse me, I mean Mademoiselle Cinderella." He winked.

Val's mother whispered something into her daughter's ear that made Val light up in a way Ella hadn't seen before. Then the three grown-ups walked off into the crowd to explore the festival.

"Let's put on a show!" Val called to Ella. Within minutes, the girls had small crowds of children gathered in front of their booths. And put on a show they did.

Ella used her puppets to tell a story of a maiden who had fallen into a deep, dreamy sleep. When she awoke, she was lost in a strange forest. She searched and searched for a way out but only became more lost. She called out for help, and the only one who answered her was a well-dressed frog. When the maiden asked for directions, the frog danced a jig.

When the maiden asked his name, the frog spun in circles. When the maiden began to cry, the frog hopped and skipped. Through the maiden's tears, the frog continued to dance. The maiden became so tired of being sad that she decided to join him. The maiden and the frog danced and danced until the maiden began to laugh. A fairy appeared. She told the maiden that a terrible witch had cursed the frog, forcing him to do nothing but dance alone for years until he found a partner. The maiden had broken the spell with her dance. The fairy said that since the spell was broken, she would give the maiden three choices. She could turn the frog into a gentleman to keep the maiden company in the forest. She could turn the frog into a large bird to fly the maiden home. Or she could banish the frog and put a spell on the maiden to allow her to sleep and live in her dreams forever.

The maiden looked at the frog, who had helped her find laughter in a time of sorrow. She told the fairy she would not make a choice. She would rather keep the frog just the way he was. In the blink of an eye, the maiden found herself back home, the frog by her side. And they lived out the rest of their days as the very best of friends.

The children loved it. They had laughed, clapped, oohed, and aahed at all the right parts. As soon as that show ended, a new crowd formed to watch the next one.

Val's show seemed to be going just as well. Ella was too busy with her own show to watch, but she could hear children squealing with delight at Val's wacky-looking puppets. Everything was going just as the girls had hoped.

Throughout the day, Ella noticed a man walking back and forth between the puppet booths. Because of the chill she felt as he paused in front of her show, she was sure it was Sir Edgard. He was tall, with a pair of spectacles that seemed much too small on top of his protruding nose. He wore fine clothes, although they seemed dark and heavy for such a bright summer day.

Ella tried to ignore the anger she felt when she saw him, thinking of poor Claudio hiding back in the shack. As she continued dancing her puppets across the stage, it struck her: maybe Sir Edgard had something good in him, too. As her father had said, there was something good in everyone—and he had been more than right about Val.

Though the day was long, as all summer days are, before Ella knew it, the sun began to set. The festival torches lining the village were lit, including one behind Val's booth. Ella stepped away from her last show just in time to see the lighting of the grand bonfire in the center of the village square. The gathered crowd roared with applause. Ella felt her face brighten in the glow of the flames. The judging ceremony would begin at any moment, as it always did at sundown.

Ella glanced at Val to see if she'd noticed the fire. Ella was ready to call her over, but Val was rummaging around in her cart, looking for something.

Ella started toward Val's booth to offer a hand when Val shot up, holding a large piece of cloth. It was one of the curtains that used to hang in her shack to hide her puppets.

"Everyone!" Val clapped her hands loudly three times, drawing the attention of the

bonfire crowd. "Mademoiselle Valentine has one last show!" Val draped the curtain across the front of her puppet booth and disappeared behind it with a torch.

What could she possibly be doing? Ella wondered. This must be the trick Val had promised.

A shadow moved behind the curtain. It was dark and strong against the white cloth. Ella recognized the shape. It was one of Val's puppets, a long-limbed creature that looked like a cross between a spider and a hare. The shadowed limbs began to move, and Val's voice boomed into the crowd. She told a story about how the creature came to life.

Several more puppets appeared behind the curtain, all in shapes Ella recognized. None of the beautiful details—the metalwork or the clever use of flowers and trinkets—could be seen. In their place was something new: another level of puppetry and creation. Val had not only made puppets; she had made shadow puppets, using the Midsummer Festival torches as her stage lights. The audience was in awe of the shadow show, and Ella was, too.

When Val's performance was over, the crowd erupted in applause, whistles, and cheers. Val came out and took a bow, sneaking a grin at Ella. Ella grinned back. Val was right. She had had a trick, and there was no doubt in Ella's mind that she had won the contest. But before she could walk over to congratulate her, the trumpets sounded. The judging was about to begin.

All the puppeteers stood in front of their booths, their puppets lying limply on the small stages. Sir Edgard paced in front of them, back and forth, back and forth. He cradled the gold coin on his palm, its brilliance shining in the crackling light of the bonfire. When he reached Val's booth the third time, Ella puffed up her chest, ready to explode with cheers.

But Sir Edgard kept walking. He stopped between Val's and Ella's booths. He took a great dramatic pause as he faced the crowd, holding the gold coin up for everyone to see. "Ladies and gentlemen, your winner!" he announced.

And he grabbed Ella's hand and raised it in victory.

Chapter 10
An Important Voice

Ella couldn't believe her ears or the fact that her arm was raised in the air. She let her hand fall out of Sir Edgard's, only to see it holding the gold coin he had pressed into her palm. It was strange. Ella was holding the coin she'd been dreaming of in the garden for so long. But now it felt like a heavy stone in her hand.

"Congratulations," Sir Edgard said.

Ella was so stunned, she hadn't noticed that the crowd was clapping—clapping very politely. Ella was sure they knew, as she knew, that the wrong person had won. This didn't feel like victory to Ella. This should have been Val's victory.

Ella glanced over at her friend, expecting to see her upset. But she wasn't. Val was clapping louder and harder than anyone else, her face full of pride and true joy.

Ella looked up at Sir Edgard, who was nodding at the crowd. His face was pinched in an awkward smile. "But, sir," Ella began. "Surely, sir . . . did you miss Val, I mean,

Mademoiselle Valentine's show? How is it possible that she's not the winner?"

Sir Edgard cleared his throat. "I saw that child's puppets. They're not what this fine tradition is about. Fancy tricks like that light show can't disguise what those puppets are made of. . . . Garbage, scraps, nothing more." He spoke his words with such confidence and authority, Ella could have almost believed him. Almost, if she didn't know Val.

But she did know Val.

And Ella knew what to do. She felt her spirit return as she looked at her friend. She took a step toward Val, thinking about what she would name the goat, the first animal for her family's farm. But before Ella got very far, she was stopped in her tracks. A voice called out over the noise of the crowd. An important voice.

The voice of the King.

Chapter 11
A Message from the King

Not even in her daydreams had Ella pictured this: approaching her was the King. She fell into a deep curtsy.

"A marvelous show, child. Please, please, stand," the King said.

Ella did as he asked. "Thank you, Your Majesty," she said. She tried to look at him but was too nervous to meet his eyes. She looked at the top of his crown instead.

She'd never seen such gleaming gold or sparkling jewels. This would fuel her daydreams for a very long time.

"Congratulations on all your hard work." The King nodded at Ella and walked away.

Ella's breath caught in her throat. Could that really have happened? Words exchanged with the King? She saw her parents standing back in the crowd. Their eyes met, and Ella smiled.

"And you, young lady," the King said. The King was still talking! Ella turned sharply to see whom he was addressing, and everyone in the crowd did, too.

Val. He was walking over to Val! Ella saw

her friend's face turn pink as she realized the King was speaking to her. She curtsied, too, so deeply that it looked like her knees might touch the cobblestones.

"Thank you, child." The King held out a hand and helped Val stand. "You had a magnificent show as well. Like nothing I've ever seen before."

Ella thought Val's eyes were going to pop out of her head. Val was speechless for the first time since Ella had met her.

The King turned to face the crowd. "It has given me great joy to see you all here at the Midsummer Festival today. This is one of my favorite celebrations of the year.

It fills my heart with pride to see what these children can do when they set their minds to it. Did everyone get a chance to see the puppet shows?"

The crowd whooped and applauded in response.

The King smiled. "I think what we've seen today, and especially this evening, demonstrates why our kingdom is one of the proudest and strongest in all the land. For years we've relied upon the talents of the cleverest and the brightest of our people. They don't spend our wealth on outside extravagance, but instead they build upon the rich resources we have here." The King put a hand on Val's shoulder. "This girl is a fine example of one of those people, the kind who have made this village and this king-dom as prosperous as it is today."

Ella wanted to run over to Val, grab her hand, and jump in delight at the King's praise. But she couldn't, as the King had Val's full attention. Ella watched Sir Edgard instead. His face turned a shade of dark crimson.

"Young lady." The King knelt down before Val.

"Mademoiselle Valentine," Val said.

The King let out an uproarious laugh.

Val smiled.

"Mademoiselle Valentine. I would be very grateful, and proud, if you would let me keep your puppets in the castle. I think they'd be wonderful entertainment for visitors from other kingdoms. Not to mention, I'd like to show them what a lucky king I am to have such brilliant subjects." The King reached into his pocket. "This would be for a small fee, of course."

Val put her hand to her mouth and then quickly uncovered it. "Oh, yes, Your Majesty! I'd be honored!"

The King dropped a velvet pouch into Val's hands. Ella could hear the clinking of coins as it fell. Coins just like the one still warm in Ella's hand, but many, many more.

"Enjoy the bonfires, everyone!" The King waved at his subjects. Then, with his guards at his side, he disappeared into the crowd.

Ella ran over to Val and wrapped her in her arms. There was no doubt in her mind. Dreams were real, and they were coming true right now.

Chapter 12
A Rainbow of Dreams

Ella lounged on the garden bench, staring into the treetops and singing softly. She wasn't singing so the fairies would listen. She was singing so her heart would have a voice. She felt so full of happiness, full of wonder, and full of dreams come true. But stitched through these feelings was also a thread of sadness. In a few minutes she would be walking to the village to say goodbye to her friend.

As it turned out, the gold the King had given Val, together with Val's mother's savings, was enough for them to buy a small farm out in the country. Ella was amazed at how right her own mother had been. Val's dreams had made magic happen and had shown Ella that what she felt in the garden was true: anything was possible.

"Would you like me to come with you, darling?" Ella heard her mother's voice behind her and smiled as she turned her head from the sky.

"I'll be all right, Mother. Bruno will be with me," Ella said as she stood.

"It's never easy to say goodbye to a friend. Especially one as wonderful and new as Val," Ella's mother said.

"No. I don't expect it will be. But I feel that it's not goodbye. Even if she's leaving . . . I know she's not really leaving me." Ella looked into her mother's eyes. "Does that sound like nonsense?"

Ella's mother shook her head. "Not even a bit."

"Come, Bruno!" At Ella's call, Bruno tore himself away from playing with the chickens and raced over.

Ella had just started for the village path

when she felt something placed in her hand. It was her mother's fan. "It's warm out here, Ella," her mother said. "Look after yourself."

Ella gripped the fan, opening it once and folding it up again. She'd always adored this fan. Its elegant beauty was so much like her mother's. "Thank you, Mother. I will," Ella said, kissing her on the cheek.

Ella and Bruno made their way toward the edge of the village, where the road into the western country began. Val and her mother were there, sorting and arranging their few belongings in a covered wagon they'd hired for their journey. The wagon was larger than Ella had expected. She

peeked inside to find cages of chickens, three pigs, two sheep, and a goose. And to her surprise, behind the wagon were two cows, chewing on the grass that lined the path.

"Val! There are so many animals. I thought the gold was only enough to start with the house!" Ella exclaimed.

Val hopped down from the front of the wagon. "You'll never believe it. When my mother told Sir Edgard our plan, he said there was no point for him to keep the animals without someone to look after them. So he sold them to us. All except his two prized pigs." Val lowered her voice to a whisper. "I think we may have cheated him. He took only three coins."

Ella frowned. "Sir Edgard hardly seems like the kind of man to let himself be taken advantage of. Perhaps he was being kind?"

Val thought for a moment. She lifted Claudio out of the wagon so he could say hello to Bruno, who'd been whining at her feet for the pig. "You know, when he made the deal, he did say I could keep the runt for free. So it seems he knew about Claudio all along."

"It's like my father said, Val. There's good in everyone. Even old Sir Edgard," Ella declared.

Val laughed. "Let's not get carried away."

"Everything's all set, girls. I need to run to the market for one last thing." Val's mother reached her arms out to Ella for a hug. "It's been a pleasure knowing you, Ella. Please come visit us anytime." She gave Ella a squeeze and left.

Val and Ella stood in silence. They watched Bruno and Claudio wrestle on the ground.

Val finally spoke. "It's true, you know. You can visit us anytime. I know it's not the same as walking down the path into the village, but it's only half a day's journey."

Ella nodded. "I noticed you don't have a goat in that wagon," she said.

"Oh, right. Well, we never had a goat on Sir Edgard's property. That's why I wanted one," Val said.

Ella pulled the gold coin out of her pocket. "I was hoping you might use this for a goat. For me, of course. It could be my goat. You could just look after it. And then I'd have another friend to visit."

Val beamed as she took the coin. "No dress after all?"

Ella shook her head. "A goat seems much more exciting."

Val clapped her hands. "If it's a goat you

want, then a goat you shall have!" And with that, she pulled Ella in close for a hug. They embraced for a while, and Ella felt a tear roll down her cheek. When they pulled apart, Ella could see that Val's eyes were wet, too.

"Don't be sad, Val. I'm so happy for you," Ella said, wiping away her tear.

"You've been a great friend, Ella," Val said, sniffling.